I KEPT PRESSING THE 100 MILLION BUTTON
~THE UNBEATABLE REJECT SWORDSMAN~

2

Allen Rodol

A boy who kept pressing the 100-Million-Year Button until he became the strongest swordsman in the land. He received a monthlong suspension for excessive violence at the Elite Five Holy Festival, so he's currently working as a witchblade.

"Don't tell me... is that you, Dodriel?!"

Dodriel Barton

A prodigy with the blade who attended Grand Swordcraft Academy. He disappeared after losing his duel with Allen.

"You'll spoil our special reunion... **Reject Swordsman.**"

Tirith Magdarote

The treasurer of the Student Council. Despite her gloomy disposition, she enjoys a good prank.

"Yawn... Mornin'..."

"Victory was ours for the taking!"

Lilim Chorine

A second-year at Thousand Blade. Serves as the secretary of the Student Council. Her bright and energetic personality makes her the life of the organization.

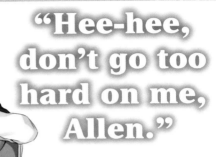

"Hee-hee, don't go too hard on me, Allen."

Shii Arkstoria

Student Council president of Thousand Blade Academy. Boasts excellent swordcraft. She is normally ladylike and mature, but the sore loser in her brings out a childish side.

"Huh? Is something wrong, Allen?"

"Look, Allen, look! It's so pretty!"

Lia Vesteria

A princess from the neighboring Vesteria Kingdom who lives in the same apartment as Allen. Her grades are excellent, and she weilds the Soul Attire Dragon King Fafnir.

"Let's get in the water. It'll be fun."

Rose Valencia

The sole inheritor of the Cherry Blossom Blade Style. Although she's among the most talented first-years, she struggles with mornings and studying.

CONTENTS

I KEPT PRESSING
THE

100-
MILLION-YEAR
BUTTON AND CAME OUT ON TOP

~THE UNBEATABLE REJECT SWORDSMAN~ 2

**SYUICHI
TSUKISHIMA**

Illustration by **MOKYU**

YEN
ON

New York

I KEPT PRESSING THE 100-MILLION-YEAR BUTTON AND CAME OUT
ON TOP: ~THE UNBEATABLE REJECT SWORDSMAN~
SYUICHI TSUKISHIMA

Translation by Luke Hutton
Cover art by Mokyu

1 OKUNEN BUTTON O RENDA SHITA ORE HA, KIZUITARA SAIKYO NI
NATTE ITA Vol.2 ~RAKUDAI KENSHI NO GAKUIN MUSO~
©Syuichi Tsukishima, Mokyu 2019
First published in Japan in 2019 by KADOKAWA CORPORATION, Tokyo.
English translation rights arranged with KADOKAWA CORPORATION, Tokyo,
through TUTTLE-MORI AGENCY, INC., Tokyo.

English translation © 2022 by Yen Press, LLC

Yen On
150 West 30th Street, 19th Floor
New York, NY 10001

Visit us at yenpress.com
facebook.com/yenpress
twitter.com/yenpress
yenpress.tumblr.com
instagram.com/yenpress

First Yen On Edition: March 2022

Yen On is an imprint of Yen Press, LLC.
The Yen On name and logo are trademarks of Yen Press, LLC.

Library of Congress Cataloging-in-Publication Data
Names: Tsukishima, Syuichi, author. | Mokyu, illustrator. | Hutton, Luke, translator.
Title: I kept pressing the 100-million-year button and came out on top /
Syuichi Tsukishima ; illustration by Mokyu ; translation by Luke Hutton.
Other titles: Ichiokunen button o renda shita ore wa, kizuitara saikyo ni natte ita.
English Description: First Yen On edition. | New York, NY : Yen On, 2021–
Identifiers: LCCN 2021034588 | ISBN 9781975322342 (v. 1 ; trade paperback) |
ISBN 9781975322366 (v. 2 ; trade paperback)
Subjects: LCGFT: Fantasy fiction. | Light novels.
Classification: LCC PL876.S857 I3413 2021 | DDC 895.6/36—dc23
LC record available at https://lccn.loc.gov/2021034588

ISBNs: 978-1-9753-2236-6 (paperback)
978-1-9753-2237-3 (ebook)

1 3 5 7 9 10 8 6 4 2

WOR

Printed in the United States of America

I KEPT PRESSING THE 100-MILLION-YEAR BUTTON AND CAME OUT ON TOP

AND CAME OUT ON TOP

~ THE UNBEATABLE REJECT SWORDSMAN ~

2

CHAPTER 1

The Witchblade Guild & the Black Organization

After my fiercely contested match with Shido Jukurius, Ice King Academy's captain at the Elite Five Holy Festival, I was checked into the hospital for an examination. The doctors ran a number of tests but found nothing wrong with me. I was the very picture of health.

My stay ended up being pretty brief, so I joined up with Lia and Rose as soon as the hospital released me. They were both thrilled to see that I was okay, and they even held a modest party to celebrate my discharge from the hospital. It was a nice, leisurely time.

The following day, we joined back up to gather in front of the Thousand Blade Academy chairwoman's office. We were there to speak to Chairwoman Reia.

I knocked on the black-painted door three times.

"Enter."

I heard the chairwoman's businesslike voice through the door. I was amazed she could sound so dignified while accomplishing no work whatsoever. I didn't think a man could have pulled that off.

"Excuse us," I announced.

We gently opened the door and entered the room.

"Oh, it's you three…"

Reia was sitting in her black office chair, engrossed in a copy of *Weekly Shonen Blade*.

"Good morning, Chairwoman," I greeted.

"Morning. Are you feeling okay?" she asked me.

"Yes. They performed a number of examinations on me but found nothing wrong."

"That's what I wanna hear. Okay, I want you three to get straight to work on the volunteer duty you'll be performing as punishment for violating the rules of the Holy Festival," the chairwoman told us, before clapping her hands.

But there was something I absolutely needed to ask her beforehand.

"Chairwoman, what was that...*thing*, which took over my body?"

"Hmm... Long story short, that was your Spirit Core. Lia, you've already acquired your Soul Attire; did you arrive at the same conclusion?"

Lia nodded. Reia then continued her explanation.

"A Spirit Core is a mass of power that resides within each person's soul. Everyone has a single core, and it can manifest as a variety of supernatural entities—ancestral spirits, cryptids, lost souls, etc. Soul Attire is an embodiment of a piece of the Spirit Core. Anyway, I have no doubt that your Spirit Core hijacked your body."

"When Spirit Cores take over other people, do they also end up like...like *that*?" I asked.

"In theory, yes...but there aren't many that possess such a strong enough sense of self to accomplish that. It's safe to assume that yours is special somehow."

"So my Spirit Core has a mind of his own..."

Another existence, separate from my own, lay dormant within my body. That knowledge felt indescribably strange.

"That being said, I don't think you have anything to worry about at the moment. It was in control of your body for a fairly long time; even a Spirit Core as powerful as yours must've had to expend a massive amount of energy to maintain that."

"If you say so..."

It sounded like I wasn't the only one who'd struggled when I was possessed.

"All right, let's talk about what you'll be doing during your suspension!" the chairwoman announced enthusiastically, trying to brighten the mood. "As I said the other day, you three will be working as witchblades. Your volunteer period is going to last a month. In order for this to pass as punishment, you are forbidden from accepting rewards."

She paused briefly.

"First, head to the Aurest Branch of the Witchblade Guild. The chief there is an old acquaintance of mine. I've already spoken to him, so I'm sure the transition will be smooth. Rose, do you mind showing them the way?" Reia asked, looking at Rose.

"No problem," she replied curtly.

Why did she ask Rose?

While I mulled that over, Rose took from her pocket a metal plate that had been engraved with *Rose Valencia* and what looked like a registration number. It must have been a witchblade identification badge.

"As you can see, I'm already a witchblade. I'm not currently active, but I've worked for the guild before," she told us casually.

"That's right. Rose is your senior in this area by many years. If you have any problems, just ask her for help," the chairwoman added.

And thus, we'd settled on heading to the Aurest Witchblade Guild.

"See you later, Chairwoman Reia!" I said.

"I pray that this will be a beneficial experience for you all!" she responded.

Lia, Rose, and I then departed Thousand Blade Academy.

■

Allen, Lia, and Rose left the chairwoman's office.

"Eighteen," Reia muttered.

"Yes, ma'am! Do you require something, Mistress Reia?"

He quickly lifted his head from the work he had been performing silently in the corner of the room.

"I want you to serve as Allen's bodyguard."

"His bodyguard? Understood."

Swiftly picking up on what she was implying, he politely nodded.

"Two of the chairs pushed strongly for Allen's expulsion, and if Ferris is to be believed, they even tried to bribe the other two chairs to go along with them," Reia noted.

"How terrible."

That was new information to Eighteen. This job was going to be more dangerous than he'd initially suspected.

"I think it's more than likely they'll send an assassin after him. If any suspicious characters draw near Allen, take them out immediately. Your Soul Attire is a little dangerous, but...I grant you special permission to use it in this case."

"Yes, ma'am...but are you sure this is okay?" he asked with timid concern after receiving her order.

"What do you mean?"

"If I'm not here, then who will get the work done...?"

"Ah, that is an issue... I also grant you special permission to take paperwork with you. Keep at them while you watch over Allen."

"...Yes, ma'am," Eighteen consented reluctantly, realizing that he would now have to contend with the difficult task of guarding Allen and doing the chairwoman's work at the same time.

"Mistress Reia, may I ask a question?"

"What is it?"

"Acting as Master Allen's guard inevitably means that I will be tailing Lady Lia and Lady Rose as well."

"Naturally."

Duh. What's he getting at? thought Reia. She waited for him to continue.

"They're both so very attractive... Um, this is hard to say, but..."

Eighteen was unusually tongue-tied.

"Spit it out, man!" Reia shouted, irritated.

"Well... If a chance were to arise, would it be okay for me to sneak a peep?"

With effort, he forced himself to voice his desire.

"How stupid are you? Of course you can't do that. No way."

"Grrr... U-understood."

And so, Eighteen would have to grapple with the three harsh tasks of protecting Allen, doing Reia's desk work, and suppressing his urges.

■

We followed Rose through the streets of Aurest. About ten minutes after we left Thousand Blade Academy, a building came into view that looked like it might be our destination.

"We're here."

As I expected, Rose came to a sudden halt in front of the structure that I'd had my eye on.

"I-is this the Witchblade Guild...?"

"Th-this is a joke, right...?"

It was a large, three-story edifice that had almost certainly gone decades without repair. Wind and rain had worn down its brick exterior, and colorful graffiti covered the walls. In short, the office was a blight on the area's scenery.

Maybe witchblades really are a bunch of brutes...

Holy knights were serious and honest, while witchblades were frivolous and insincere—that was the reputation both professions had in society.

I thought that image was born of past discrimination and prejudice.

Looking at this building, though, I couldn't help but think that stereotype was spot-on.

Lia and I recoiled from the run-down state of the exterior.

"What's wrong? Are you not coming in?" Rose asked, looking as relaxed as someone returning home. She didn't seem perturbed by the building at all.

"H-hey, Rose... Is this actually the Witchblade Guild?"

It wasn't surprising to see Lia react so negatively. She was a princess, after all.

"Yeah, of course."

Baffled, Rose reached for the door. Lia and I locked eyes and nodded.

"I—I guess we have no choice but to go in..." I sighed.

"Y-yeah... Let's do it," agreed Lia.

Although there was a chance that the inside of the building could be surprisingly nice despite its run-down exterior, it only took two seconds for that delusion to be shattered.

"Wh-what the...?!"

"It stinks!"

When we opened the door, the thick stench of alcohol immediately assaulted our nostrils. The interior seemed to double as a bar, and despite it being noon, many people were already sharing drinks.

This fits the stereotype exactly... Actually, it's twice as bad.

Lia must have been thinking the exact same thing; her disgust showed openly on her beautiful face.

"*Hic*, who the hell're you kids...? I've never seen ya 'round 'ere."

A witchblade, who was clearly plastered, approached us.

"...Lia, Rose, get behind me," I told them quietly, stepping in front of them.

"Wait a damn sec... *Hic*, you two ladies are fiiiine. How'd ya like a round with me...?"

The man staggered unsteadily toward us.

...I need to get us out of here.

"I'm sorry, but we have business here," I answered.

Standing between him and the girls, I politely shot him down.

"Tch, no one caaaares whatcha hafta shay, ya little brrrat!"

He swung the alcohol bottle in his hand down upon my head. The bottle smashed to pieces upon contact, drenching me in beer from head to toe.

"A-are you okay, Allen?! What do you think you're doing?!!" Lia yelled at the man.

"You've had too much to drink!" scolded Rose.

They two of them barred his way.

"*Pfft*... Gah-ha-ha-ha, what a loser! You're shoaked!"

The drunken man grabbed his belly and guffawed mockingly.

"You prick!"

"You've gone way too far!"

Evidently, he'd crossed a line for Lia and Rose, because they both reached for the swords at their hips.

"I'm fine. Calm down," I quickly said to stop them.

"How could we calm down?!"

"He smashed a bottle on your head!"

"Remember that we're suspended. If we cause trouble here, we'd be inconveniencing the chairwoman. Besides, all he did was get me wet."

It would be exhausting if I went around getting angry at every little indignity.

"What do you mean?"

"Y-you're not hurt?"

"Yeah, I'm fine. See?"

I lightly swept the glass shards off my head and showed them that I was unharmed.

"Th-that's impossible!"

"You don't have a single cut!"

That's right—I was totally uninjured. The only inconvenience I'd suffered was being drenched with beer. He'd probably eased off before striking me with the bottle.

"Anyway, let's get moving," I suggested.

"S-sure..."

"If you insist, Allen..."

We passed by the drunk and headed for the reception desk. The other witchblades in the guild, who had been watching surreptitiously, started to jeer.

"They're totally ignoring you, Dred!"

"Gah-ha-ha-ha! You got embarrassed by three little kids! Who's the loser now?!"

"You're a disgrace to all witchblades!"

As his peers mocked him, Dred turned red in the face and trembled.

...These people were obnoxious.

"You little brat!"

His ego grievously wounded, Dred yanked his sword from his hip. "Don't think you can get away with making a fool of me!"

He swung his weapon three times and pointed its tip at me.

Now this *I can't ignore.*

I stared directly into his eyes and spoke.

"Swordcraft isn't child's play. Are you...*sure* you want to do this?"

A blade wielder brandished their weapon to fight. I was confirming that this was what the man wanted.

"U-uh..."

Dred's face quickly went pale, and he took two steps back.

Holy cow...I-I've never seen Allen act so menacing! thought Lia.

His malice is so overwhelming! thought Rose.

A few seconds later...

"S-sorry about that. I clearly got too inebriated, but I've come to my senses now... Please forgive me," the man begged before sheathing his sword and bowing deeply.

"Apology accepted. Make sure to drink responsibly, okay?" I responded.

I decided to let it go. Everyone makes mistakes; I had made countless in my life. Most importantly, no damage had come of this. I just reeked a little.

"S-sure thing. Thank you! I'll treat you to a round next time!"

The man hurriedly left the Witchblade Guild as soon as he said that. I appreciated the sentiment, but I was underage. I couldn't have alcohol.

Seems like he wasn't so bad after all, I thought.

"A-Allen..."

Lia called my name, sounding slightly hoarse. There was fear in her eyes. Due to her royal upbringing, she'd probably never experienced anything like that.

"Are you okay, Lia? Do you want to rest somewhere?" I asked.

"N-no, I'm fine. That just startled me a bit," she answered.

"If you're sure... Don't hesitate to tell me if you're not feeling great."

"O-okay! Thanks, Allen!"

Thank goodness... He's back to his nice and normal self, she thought.

Advancing farther into the now dead-silent Witchblade Guild, we found an area labeled RECEPTION in large letters and hesitated when we saw a rather scary-looking man sitting behind the desk.

I-is he really the receptionist...?

He had a shiny bald head and a neat mustache. His sunglasses were blacker than black, and his brawny body bulged with muscles. I guessed he was in his midforties. He was reading a newspaper, his face as expressionless as could be.

I-is there another clerk anywhere?

I quickly looked around but didn't see anyone else who fit the bill.

Guess he's the only one...

Although I was scared to talk to him, Chairwoman Reia had told us she'd spoken to the branch chief, so I didn't think there would be a problem...or at least, I *hoped* there wouldn't be a problem.

I gulped loudly, then took one step forward—but Lia and Rose grabbed my clothes and tugged me back.

"Y-you can't, Allen! That guy is clearly dangerous!" warned Lia.

"You should stay away from him. He's got the face of a murderer," cautioned Rose.

"I don't see anyone else, though...," I responded.

The Witchblade Guild was a public institution. This guy worked for the state, so I figured he should be decent enough. I was still scared to approach him, but we couldn't just stand around doing nothing.

"...Let's go."

"You're actually going to talk to him?!" exclaimed Lia.

"Okay. Let me prepare myself...," responded Rose.

We worked up the necessary determination and stood before him.

"What do you want?"

He folded the newspaper he was reading, then calmly stood up.

H-he's huge!! thought Allen.

I-is he man or bear?! wondered Lia.

He couldn't look more brutish..., noted Rose.

The man was around 198 centimeters tall, and though he was just a bit shorter than Ms. Paula, his appearance was incredibly intimidating. He was scary in an entirely different way than she was. Despite my fear, I summoned up some courage and forced myself to address him.

"U-um—"

"I saw that just now… You're *good*, kid," he acknowledged, his fiendish face twisting. That was probably his way of smiling, but it was terrifying, nevertheless.

"Th-thanks…"

I didn't know what he was praising me for, but I thought I should go ahead and take the compliment.

"I haven't seen you three in here before. You wouldn't happen to be the volunteers my old pal Reia told me about, would you?"

"…! Y-yes, we are!"

I saw a light at the end of the tunnel.

"I knew it! I'm glad I noticed you. All she told me on the phone was that 'three strangers are going to arrive at your guild to work as volunteers, so please take care of them.' That's not much to go on… She hung up on me right after that and wouldn't pick up the damn phone when I called back. I didn't have a clue what she was talkin' about," he admitted, scratching his bald head.

"S-sorry about our teacher…"

Honestly, I really did feel for him there.

"Ha-ha, don't worry 'bout it. She's always been like *that*… Ah, I haven't introduced myself. I'm Bonz. Bonz Daulton. I'm the branch chief of the Aurest Witchblade Guild. Nice to meetcha."

He held out his right hand and gave us each a handshake. He might have looked scary, but he didn't seem like a bad person. The three of us gave a simple self-introduction.

"I'm Allen Rodol. I'm looking forward to working with you."

"I am Lia Vesteria. Nice to meet you."

"I'm Rose Valencia. Pleasure."

"Allen, Lia, and Rose, the Bounty Hunter… All right, I won't forget it."

Mr. Bonz nodded as he matched our names to our faces.

"Let's start by getting your witchblade registration out of the way. You two are the only ones who need it, right?" he asked, eyeing Lia and me.

""Yes,"" we both answered.

"Fill these out with your name, age, address, and whatnot."

He held out two pieces of paper labeled *Applicant Registration*. Lia and I answered the required fields.

"I'm done."

"Finished."

There was surprisingly little to write down. They only requested the bare minimum of personal information here.

"All right, lemme see 'em."

Mr. Bonz took off his pitch-black sunglasses and put on some reading glasses. His eyes looked surprisingly friendly.

"Good, you didn't miss anything."

After checking our forms, he put away his reading glasses and switched back to his intimidating shades.

"I'm gonna make your badges, so wait here a moment."

"Yes, sir."

He disappeared deeper into the reception area. We let out a collective sigh of relief as soon as he did so.

"Haah... He looks terrifying, but he's a good guy on the inside. Thank goodness," I said.

"Yeah, and he has really cute eyes, too," agreed Lia.

"Goes to show you can't judge someone by how they look...," said Rose, nodding.

Lia and Rose both concurred as well.

As we waited for Mr. Bonz to make our badges, another scuffle broke out.

"Say that one more time, you asshole!!!"

"I'll say it as many times as I need! It was entirely your fault that we failed this job!"

Two men, who must have been in the same party, seemed on the verge of coming to blows. The dark red of their faces made it clear even from a distance that they were dead-drunk.

"Geez, another brawl..."

"I wonder if all Witchblade Guilds are this dangerous."

"From my experience, I think this one's a little worse than usual..."

We spoke in hushed tones as we watched the scene unfold.

"Yeah, fight, fight, fight!!"

"Get on with it! I'm starving!"

The surrounding witchblades began to shout as they urged the two participants on. Apparently, they thought a rumble would make for good drinking entertainment.

"Good lord, do they have to be so loud...?"

Mr. Bonz clicked his tongue loudly as he emerged from the back of the reception area with two badges in hand.

"M-Mr. Bonz, those two guys just started going at it," Lia said quickly, and he nodded.

"Yeah, I know. Wait a sec."

He headed over toward them; as the branch chief, it was probably his job to break up fights. However, the men were too engrossed in their heated punching match to notice his approach.

"GO TO HELL!"

"Heh, nice miss, you goddamn idiot!"

The two intoxicated witchblades raised their fists.

"Guys, is my guild really the best place to duke it out?"

"...?!"

Their faces both went pale upon hearing Mr. Bonz's deep, chilling voice.

"M-Mr. Bonz?! We were just, uh..."

"Th-this isn't a fight! We're only messing around!"

Clearly terrified, they put their arms around each other's shoulders in false amity.

"Good lord...I trust you two know the rules of the Aurest Guild?"

"No, please, not the fist... Anything but the fist... Bwuh?!"

Mr. Bonz threw a merciless right-handed straight into one of their faces.

"Ouch…"

"That was a haymaker…"

Lia and Rose both flinched back from the sight of that punch.

What a strike…

The transfer of weight from his legs to his back, from his back to his chest, and from his chest to his arms had been flawless. His right fist had traveled in a perfectly straight line, without the slightest hint of wavering. That punch was practically a work of art.

The other man stepped back after witnessing such a horrifying blow right beside him.

"I-I'm sorry! He started it by calling me a burden!" he screamed, simultaneously groveling and making excuses for himself.

"Come on, man, you know better. Both sides are guilty in a brawl. That means you both get socked."

"N-no, please… Gu-hah!"

He slugged the second man's face with a straight just as beautiful as the last one. After bringing the fight to an end, Mr. Bonz raised his voice for the entire guild to hear.

"I expect every single one of you to drink in moderation, not act like drunken oafs. Got it?!"

All the witchblades in the guild, which was now totally silent, nodded. With his work done, Mr. Bonz returned to us.

"Haah… Sorry 'bout that. We get a lot of rowdy drinkers around here. I can't even tell you how many times that happens a day."

"R-really…?"

It sounded like he had his work cut out for him.

Clearing his throat with a cough, he returned to the previous topic.

"This badge is your identification as a witchblade. Make sure you don't lose it."

""Yes, sir! Thank you!"" Lia and I both replied.

The badges had a few red specks on them; it was probably blood from when Mr. Bonz had pummeled the two sloshed men.

"" ""...""

After witnessing that powerful right-handed straight, though, neither of us was going to mention it.

"So what's the plan? Gonna take some jobs?"

"Y-yes, we would like that," I answered.

"I see... Can you fill me in on what's happenin' here first, though? Why are you three volunteering?"

Oh yeah, the chairwoman didn't properly explain the situation.

"Hmm, where to start...?"

I gave a summary of the events that had brought us here.

I told him how I'd ended up in a literal battle to the death against my opponent in the Elite Five Holy Festival; that I'd been suspended from the academy for one month as punishment; that Lia and Rose had been similarly reprimanded to take collective responsibility; and that while we couldn't go to class, Chairwoman Reia had "disciplined" us in a way that would keep our sword skills from growing rusty, which consisted of taking on assignments as witchblades without compensation.

Mr. Bonz listened quietly while seated in his chair.

"I see, so that's what happened..." He nodded as if satisfied. "If that's why you're here, I recommend you take monster-extermination jobs!"

"Monsters? Not beasts?" I asked.

Beast exterminations covered wild bears, wolves, and other animals that occasionally attacked humans but didn't go out of their way to do so. By contrast, monster exterminations concerned chimeras, ogres, and other dangerous creatures that actively targeted people.

"Of course! Beast killing would hardly make for good training! A real swordfighter should take on the thrill of hunting monsters!"

He put three request sheets on the desk. They were hunts for goblins, ogres, and a chimera, respectively. These were the requests he was recommending we undertake.

"B-but Chairwoman Reia recommended beast exterminations..."

"Ah, pay that no mind. That Reia is hopeless... Can't remember the difference between beasts and monsters no matter how many times I tell her…," Mr. Bonz replied wistfully, almost gazing off into the distance.

…Just what kind of relationship did these two have?

I was a little curious, but I didn't want to upset him by asking something so intrusive, so I refrained.

"Allen, what should we do? I've hunted goblins before in Vesteria…," Lia told me.

"Chimeras are strong, but the three of us should be able to handle one…I think," ventured Rose.

They both stared at me silently. They were giving me the right to choose.

Goblins, ogres, and a chimera…

Since I'd never fought any of them, I didn't have any useful input. Lia, though, had apparently hunted goblins in Vesteria, and Rose reckoned we could handle a chimera if we worked together.

…Might as well give it a try.

Mr. Bonz was waiting eagerly for us to accept the assignments. I didn't feel like refusing was an option.

"All right, we'll take the jobs."

"That's what I wanna hear! These three are yours!"

He stamped each of the request sheets with a large seal.

We were ready to take on our first witchblade monster exterminations.

■

After exiting the Witchblade Guild, we examined the three job sheets.

"We've got goblins, ogres, and a chimera… I know a little about each from hearsay and picture books, but I've never seen any of them in person," I admitted.

Lia and Rose looked at each other in surprise.

"Really? I've heard that monster numbers have been increasing lately. I'm pretty sure you're likely to spot any of them on the highways these days," responded Lia.

"Oh yeah, I've been hearing that rumor, too," I said.

It must have been down to good luck that I had never seen one before.

"Allen, were you noble born?" Rose asked, puzzled.

She must have assumed that because I'd told her that I'd never encountered a monster. In reality, it wasn't a sheltered upbringing that had prevented me from ever seeing one, but the fact that I'd grown up in the middle of nowhere.

"No, I was born in Goza Village. It's as rural a place as you could imagine."

"Goza Village? Sorry, I've never heard of it."

"Ah-ha-ha, that's not surprising."

My hometown was tiny, with a population of less than one hundred. Other than government officials and merchants who traded there, I doubted anyone knew it existed. That was how insignificant and economically inconsequential it was. It made sense that Rose hadn't heard of it.

I coughed to clear my throat, then brought the conversation back on track.

"Anyway, what's the plan? Should we start with the goblins?" I asked.

The task was to exterminate five of them. That was the most monsters of any of the jobs; goblins weren't very strong individually. This was probably going to be the easiest of the three.

"Yeah, I think it would make sense to warm up with the weakest monsters and then move on to the ogres," said Lia.

"I agree. Chimeras are the strongest, so it would be best to leave it for last," concurred Rose, nodding.

The three of us were on the same page.

"You can find all these monsters in Zoll Forest. Mr. Bonz probably chose these requests to make things easier for us," I guessed.

Giving us three tasks in the same area would help us cut down on travel time significantly, so I was very grateful for that.

"He's a really nice person inside despite his looks, isn't he?" noted Lia.

"Ha, his adorable eyes give him away," joked Rose.

We headed for Zoll Forest, south of Aurest.

■

We arrived at Zoll Forest after about an hour of jogging and started searching for goblins straight away. Many dangerous monsters besides goblins lurked amid these trees, so we made sure to proceed quietly.

"Allen, look!" Lia noted quietly, pointing at some hoof prints on the ground.

"Are those goblin tracks?" I asked.

"Yeah, they are," answered Lia.

"They're fresh... That means they're close," informed Rose.

"Okay. Be careful."

We moved as quietly as possible as we tracked our targets. It took about two minutes to find them.

"...There they are."

Ahead of us, I spotted seven goblins. They were bipedal, muscular creatures with green skin, each standing at about ninety centimeters tall. Rough wooden clubs hung from their hips. Fortunately, they hadn't noticed us—their attention was devoted entirely to the fruit they were greedily devouring.

"I'd like to just take them all out immediately, but...that would defeat the purpose, wouldn't it?" I asked.

"Yeah, we're here to train," responded Lia.

"We should fight them fair and square," said Rose.

Indeed, we had picked up these assignments to hone our skills. Just hunting goblins wasn't the point; what we were truly after was authentic combat experience.

"Lia, Rose, are the two of you ready?"

"Yes."

"Always."

After they gave the go-ahead, I used my sword to shake a nearby thicket. All our opponents reacted to the rustling sound at once and looked toward us.

"Ge-kya!"

"Koo-gya-gya!"

"Gya-gya-gya!"

The goblins cried out with hoarse voices, before all seven of them rushed at us simultaneously. Lia and Rose took their stances, while I prepared a long-distance attack to restrain the enemy's movement.

"First Style—Flying Shadow!"

That was the first Flying Shadow I'd used in a few days.

"...Huh?"

And somehow, it was three times stronger and faster than usual.

"Ge-hiiiii?!"

"Boo-hya?!"

"Gu-hyaaa?!"

My move sliced all seven goblins in two, bringing the engagement to a close.

"H-huh..."

Obviously, we gained no training from that.

"Uh, Allen...?"

"What was that...?"

They both gaped at me, bewildered.

"Uh, sorry...I didn't mean to finish them off so quickly," I apologized with an awkward laugh.

"No, forget that... What the heck did you just do?! That wasn't your normal Flying Shadow!"

"Was that a new move?!"

They both excitedly pressed me for an answer.

"No, that was the same old Flying Shadow..."

But somehow, the attack I'd just performed had been *three times* as powerful as my usual version. Its speed, force, and size had all been significantly greater.

What just happened?

I stared dumbfounded at my right hand.

"...We should move from this spot," Lia suggested, glancing at our slain targets.

"Yeah, good idea."

It wouldn't take long before the smell of blood attracted beasts or monsters that were stronger than the creatures that I'd just slayed. Unless we wanted to deal with them, too, we needed to move.

"Wait a sec... There we go."

With a practiced hand, Rose quickly collected a horn from each of the seven goblins.

"What are those for?"

"These are trophies to prove we killed these goblins. We can't complete the job if we don't take these back with us."

"Oh, that makes sense."

I was glad to have Rose around. Her knowledge as a former witch-blade would be invaluable.

With that, we quickly abandoned the area and began to discuss our next target.

"The ogres are next..."

The request was to fell three. Though that was fewer monsters to kill than the previous task, I still expected this job to be more difficult. Ogres were basically larger goblins. They were less intelligent than their smaller counterparts, but their size alone made them a greater threat. The height of each ogre varied, but even the small ones were as big as Ms. Paula. Put simply, they were massive.

According to rumors, some mutants even surpassed ten meters in height.

"Should we look near a body of water?" I asked.

They both nodded.

Ogres almost always lived near water because they were too unintelligent to be able to remember terrain.

If they strayed from a body of water, they wouldn't be able to find their way back. Consequently, many ogres died of thirst. That was why they would not—*could* not—leave the sources of water they'd located.

If memory served, there was a thin stream that ran south through this forest.

"How about we locate that creek and then start hunting for ogres?" I suggested.

"Sounds good to me," answered Lia.

"Sure," agreed Rose.

We headed west, and before long, we came upon a small but beautiful brook. We moved carefully upstream, until...

"*Ooorgh, ooorgh...*"

"*Voo-boo-boo...*"

"*Groor-groor...*"

...we found three ogres. They were moaning and lumbering along the riverbank, likely searching for prey.

"They're *huuuuge...*"

The ogres looked about three meters tall, and they were each gripping a large club in their right hand. They were so large that I was sure a single clean hit from them would result in serious injury or death.

Intimidated by their enormous figures, we discussed our plan in a whisper.

"We need to attack them head-on, don't we?" I asked.

"I'm a little scared, but...that's the only way we're going to get any growth out of this," said Lia, sighing.

"Ogres are dumb. If you mix in some feints, they aren't that scary," Rose assured.

She didn't seem worried about fighting ogres. That was for good reason—the skill and agility of her Cherry Blossom Blade Style would undoubtedly serve her well against the massive brutes.

"Maybe I'll...make this into a little contest of strength," I remarked.

"Hmm-hmm, I was thinking the same thing," Lia agreed with a giggle.

Honestly, I would be lying if I said I wasn't afraid...

But as a swordsman, I was curious to see how my arm strength would fare against the might of an ogre.

"I won't try to stop you two, but make sure to go on the defensive quickly if you sense you're going to be overpowered, okay?" Rose warned us with a sigh.

"Okay. I'll be careful," I reassured.

"I just wanna see what will happen. There's no need to worry," added Lia.

Once we were ready, I threw a nearby pebble at one of the ogres.

"Bwah?"

The one that I hit in the back of the head turned around to face us, and the other two followed suit. We locked eyes with them, and their faces twisted into grins. They'd finally spotted the prey they were looking for.

"They're coming!"

"Okay!"

"I'm ready!"

We each took our battle formations.

"Orrrgh... Ooooorrrgh!"

"Groaaaarrrr!"

"Gwooooohhhh!"

The monsters charged at us together. Despite their large size, they were surprisingly nimble. Those giant bodies had to be composed of muscle rather than fat.

"Let's see which of us is stronger... Come at me!"

I held the middle stance and waited for it to approach.

"Raaaaaah!"

"Hah!"

My sword collided with one of the creatures' clubs...

"Bwoh?!"

...and I easily bested its strength, sending it flying backward.

"...Huh?"

The ogre hit the back of its head hard and blacked out. I stared at it in confusion.

"Hegemonic Style—Hard Strike!"

"Cherry Blossom Blade Style—Sakura Flash!"

Lia's bout of strength with the ogre she faced ended in a tie, and then she used her Soul Attire to burn it to ashes. Meanwhile, Rose used her elegant swordcraft to kill her ogre without issue. I approached them after we successfully vanquished our targets.

"Nice job. You both did really well."

"Thank you... Though, I don't know what to think about this," said Lia.

"Where in the world did this muscle come from, Allen?" asked Rose.

They both stared at my body.

"I spent the last few days in a hospital bed; I should have weakened if anything...," I responded.

Besting that ogre had been far too easy. Maybe it had just been the weakest of the three?

Our monster hunt was going surprisingly smoothly. Mr. Bonz had been right to tell us to choose monster extermination over beast extermination.

Next, we headed toward the location of our final hunt—the chimera. Unlike the first two assignments, the exact location of its nest was indicated on the request document.

We walked toward this spot carefully, so as not to attract any troublesome monsters or beasts. Then after crossing a stream, passing through a small pond, and trekking along an animal trail, we finally located it.

"...There it is."

The chimera stood right in the middle of a slightly elevated plateau.

Chimeras were a combination of three different animals—a lion in the front, a goat in the back (with a head included), and a snake in place of a tail. The snake was very nimble, and its fangs contained a powerful venom. Each head was capable of independent thought, so engaging with these creatures was quite tricky.

Presently, the chimera was lying comfortably on its belly atop a makeshift bed of branches and grass.

"It sure is sleeping peacefully... Is it that confident that nothing can harm it?" mused Lia.

"No, that's not it. The snake tail keeps an eye open to observe its surroundings," Rose refuted, pointing at the creature's tail. Just as she'd said, the purple snake had one eye open.

"Chimeras are much stronger than the last two monsters. We have to be careful," warned Rose.

"Have you ever fought one?" I asked.

"Yeah. That was over three years ago now, but I remember it was really strong. All three sections—the lion in the front, the goat in the back, and the snake tail—attack and defend with wills of their own. That makes it very hard to find an opening to strike," she explained.

"That sounds difficult..."

"The biggest problem is its steellike skin. You have to get really close to it to have any chance of cutting through it," she said with a grave expression.

"It can't be easy getting anywhere near that thing, though," I responded.

Monsters weren't stupid. They were fully aware of the distance they needed to keep from their opponents. That meant that the lion, the goat, and the snake would act simultaneously to prevent anyone from getting too close to the body as a whole. Even without having fought a chimera yet, I could easily tell how powerful it was.

After a lengthy discussion, we concocted a plan.

First, Lia and I, with our ability to deliver powerful attacks in close-quarters combat, would hold down the tenacious lion and goat heads. Then Rose would utilize her quick decision making to subdue the snake tail. Once that was taken care of, we would finally use our three-on-two advantage to bring it down slowly but surely.

It was a sound strategy that didn't involve fishing for risky killing blows.

"Lia, are you ready?"

"Yes, let's go on zero. Rush for the viper right after us, okay, Rose?"

"Got it."

Lia then calmly began the count.

"Three...two...one..."

Our nerves flared in anticipation of a hard battle.

"...zero!"

We dashed forward immediately.

...*Huh?*

Before I knew it, I was right in front of the chimera, its body completely open to attack. Lia and Rose were way behind me.

"*Hsss!*"

"*R-roooaaarrr?!*"

"*Maaaaa?!*"

The snake hissed at me threateningly while the lion and goat jerked awake. But it was already too late for them. I was in range for the coup de grâce.

...*I've got this!*

From this close, I could do significant damage with a single move. I swung down my brandished blade.

"Eighth Style—Eight-Span Crow!"

Eight sharp slash attacks hit the chimera instantaneously. It differed from my usual Eight-Span Crow—each individual slash was ferociously sharp, as though I'd placed my entire body and mind into my sword as I swung it.

Those eight cuts tore the chimera to pieces, slicing through it as easily as if it were made of tofu.

"Wh-what was that...?"

"You've gotta be... That's impossible!"

Lia and Rose froze in front of the dead chimera with their swords still in hand.

In the end, I'd accidentally completed our first three jobs almost entirely by myself.

■

Lia and Rose hounded me after I defeated the chimera with one—er, eight strikes.

"What did you just do, Allen?! Where did that ridiculous strength come from?!" Lia asked.

"And that lightning speed!" exclaimed Rose.

"I-I'm just as surprised by this as you are," I answered.

The speed, arm strength, and sword speed I'd just displayed were at least on par with those of Shido Jukurius, the gifted swordsman whom I'd defeated at the Holy Festival. I felt like my physical capabilities had all gone up a level.

Did I gain this strength from the experience of overcoming such a powerful swordsman at the festival? Or is this a side effect of being possessed by my Spirit Core?

Either way, I was grateful for it.

I can still get stronger!

"Urgh, I need to practice more with my Soul Attire..."

"I can't let you get any better than me..."

Both girls muttered to themselves, clenching their fists.

After completing the assignments, we returned to Mr. Bonz.

"Whoa there, you already completed three requests? You kids are good!"

Mr. Bonz, who had been absorbed in some paperwork, smiled heartily. His grin was still terrifying, but I was getting used to it little by little.

"Clearly, monster extermination was the right choice," he said.

"Yes, it made for really good training," I answered.

"Gah-ha-ha, glad to hear it! Those were just a warm-up, though. I'm gonna give you more difficult jobs from here on out."

"That would be great, Mr. Bonz."

Over the course of the next few days, we tackled a variety of assignments. Naturally, they didn't all go smoothly.

During a giant-slime extermination, Lia and Rose both ended up getting their clothes singed off. That was a rough one. I avoided disaster by lending them my jacket and shirt, but panic struck me when I realized my clothes could have smelled.

I didn't sweat that much, so they were probably fine...I hope.

It had been exactly one week since we'd started working as witchblades. People really could adjust to any circumstance. I didn't even mind the appearance of the building anymore.

There's a ton of requests available...

Lia and Rose were in the bathroom, and I was absentmindedly looking at the assignment sheets posted on the job board.

"Hey, Allen! Come over here!"

Dred called out to me, holding a small glass.

"What is it, Mr. Dred? I can't drink alcohol."

He'd been imbibing less since the incident one week ago. I hadn't seen him that wasted since.

"Heh-heh-heh, you're such a Goody Two-shoes. Come on, just sit down for a bit! There are certain things you can only discuss between men...if you know what I mean," he insinuated, twisting the corners of his mouth into a grin.

Knowing Dred, I doubted he had anything worthwhile to say...but turning him down would be rude, so I resigned myself and sat down next to him.

"So which one are you seeing?"

"...Huh?"

I didn't understand what he was asking.

"Don't dodge the question, man! I'm asking which one you're dating—Lia, with her blond hair and those big knockers, or Rose, with all her beauty and grace?!"

"Huh? I—I, uh... That's..."

I babbled incoherently in response to the unexpected question.

I-is this...guy talk? Where we talk about girls? I don't know what to say...

As if they'd been eavesdropping on us, all the surrounding witchblades I'd become acquainted with butted into the conversation.

"Allen, don't tell me...are you dating both of them?!"

"Guess girls lose it for guys as talented as you... *Argh*, I'm so jealous!"

"You may have time for both, but you've gotta have a favorite, am I right?"

"No, we should ask him how far he's made it with each of them first!"

Our chat was growing more and more confusing.

I—I need to put a stop to this...fast.

I didn't want any weird rumors to spread and cause trouble for Lia and Rose.

"U-um...I'm telling you, I'm not seeing either one of them!"

I needed to make sure the witchblades were clear on this. I would have let the gossip slide if it were just about me. They say a wonder lasts but nine days, after all; everyone here would forget about it before long. That said, I needed to stand my ground and deny anything that would cause trouble for my friends.

They didn't quite react the way I wanted, however.

"Gimme a break, Allen! You expect anyone to believe that with the amount of time you spend with them?!"

"Ha-ha, I'm not falling for that one, Allen!"

Unfortunately, they weren't taking me at my word in the slightest.

You can't reason with drunk people...

No amount of explanation or detail would get them to hear me out. After accepting that, I decided to change tactics.

"Okay, fine...but don't go spreading any strange rumors. Is that clear?" I warned them.

"Y-yeah, of course!"

"Heh-heh, it was just a joke, man..."

"No need to get so serious..."

They all looked away and said no more on the subject. They must've finally gotten the hint.

"Hey, Allen!"

"Sorry for the wait. Let's take on our next job."

Lia and Rose waved their hands and called out to me from the reception area.

"Okay, I'm coming," I responded.

After I joined them, we decided to let Mr. Bonz choose our next task.

"I'd like you to take this one next," he recommended.

"Hmm… It's an escort mission," I observed.

It was a request to accompany a merchant's carriage from the capital city of Aurest to the city of Drestia, which was known as the Merchant's Town. This was the most common type of job that witchblades performed.

"This task'll be a bit simple for you three, but I have my reasons for askin' it of you. The client is an old lady, and she has a bad back. I want some skilled witchblades to accompany her just in case anything goes wrong. Willin' to take this on?"

I glanced toward Lia and Rose, and they both nodded. We were all on the same page.

"We'd be glad to."

In Goza Village, helping one another out was our way of life. If anyone had a poor rice harvest, the other farmers would each offer to share some of their yield. The same went for poor harvests of other crops, including wheat, potatoes, and onions. We would always lend a hand to those in need.

"Fantastic! That's a load off my back!"

Mr. Bonz laughed jovially and stamped the request sheet.

"I also have another request for you. This one's from me," he noted, producing thirty thousand guld from his pocket. "Could you perform a little market research for me?"

"…Market research?"

It looked like he wanted us to fulfill some kind of errand with that money, but I couldn't imagine we would get any practice out of that.

"As you're aware, this escort duty is going to take you to Drestia."

"Yes, it will."

"Starting tomorrow, a *huuuge* three-day event called the Unity Festival is going to begin there. I want you all to buy goods at a variety of stalls and report back to me with your findings."

He handed me the thirty thousand guld.

"U-um…"

"Are you...?"

"Is this your way of ordering us to go enjoy the festival?"

Rose asked the question that was on all our minds.

"No, of course not. This festival is massively popular. I'd like you to figure out the secret behind its success. The Witchblade Guild is going to hold an event of our own in the future, you see. So don't get the wrong idea—this is a very important request," he insisted.

"I don't know...," I trailed off hesitantly.

The explanation he gave was a real stretch. It was more than obvious that he just wanted us to have some fun.

Mr. Bonz then shook his head and sighed loudly.

"Here's a piece of advice for you, Allen. Pushin' yourself to train non-stop isn't good for you. You need to give yourself breaks to recharge your mind! It's important to let loose and have some fun once in a while."

"H-huh..."

"Anyway, what I'm sayin' is—you kids have been working way too hard over the last week! Act your age for once and take a damn break!"

His true motive for the request had finally emerged.

"U-uh...," I started.

"Well, but...there's just one problem...," Lia said.

"We're suspended right now," Rose stated.

"That's why this is a request from me. If anyone gives you grief about this, just tell me who. I'll beat the hell out of 'em!" he announced, cracking his knuckles. His intensity was overwhelming.

"Y-yes, sir. Thank you."

Refusing him didn't feel like an option given how hard he was pressing us to enjoy the festival, so I decided to accept his kind offer.

"Heh-heh, I'm countin' on you kids!"

We then met up with the client, an old lady named Ms. Sandy, and departed Aurest. We chatted with Ms. Sandy on the road.

"Wow, are you three students from *the* Thousand Blade Academy?" she asked, her eyes wide with surprise.

"U-uh, well... Yes, we are," I answered.

We were currently suspended, though.

"I'll have nothing to worry about with Thousand Blade students on the job! I hope I'm not wasting your time, though. I am but a poor wheat farmer, so I don't have much to pay you with," she noted, pointing to the many bags packed with wheat in the carriage.

The sacks were nearly overflowing with threshed wheat. I'd caught a glimpse of it earlier; it was nicely colored and perfectly ripe. Top-rate stuff. I was sure it would fetch a good price.

"Ah-ha-ha, we're not doing this for money," I responded.

As volunteers, we couldn't accept monetary compensation. In fact, we actually hadn't received a single reward yet for any of the requests we'd completed.

"You know, Thousand Blade Academy is said to have fallen on hard times recently, but they were dominant back in my day."

Ms. Sandy began to recount the old times.

"Especially Black Fist Reia Lasnote! I don't know much about her, but if I recall correctly, she used the Swordless School of Swordcraft. She was truly striking… Her opponents would be unrecognizable by the time she was done with them. It was so inspiring seeing that from a girl!"

She punched her right fist through the air with a *whoosh*.

"The only student who was ever a match for her was Ferris from Ice King Academy! She never actually beat Reia, though."

"Wow, that's impressive," I said.

This was really interesting to hear. She regaled us with more stories about Thousand Blade Academy on the way, and before I knew it, we had arrived in Drestia. Fortunately, we hadn't encountered any beasts or monsters on our journey.

"We're here, Ms. Sandy. I'm glad we got here without mishap," I announced.

"Thank you for escorting me. It was a joy having someone to listen to this old lady's ramblings. This is where we— ACK?!"

She froze like a statue in the middle of her sentence.

"M-Ms. Sandy?!"

"Wh-what happened?!"

"Are you okay?!"

The three of us all called out to her simultaneously.

"M-my back…," she muttered in a strained voice, her face stiff.

She hurt her spine…

I remembered Ol' Bamboo becoming bedridden when he'd thrown out his back like it was just the previous day. He was a healthy, energetic old man, but that had rendered him immobile for a full week. Back injuries were no joke.

"L-let's go to the hospital!" I exclaimed.

"N-no, I c-can't! I p-promised to deliver this c-cargo by noon…," Ms. Sandy protested.

She had a limited window to hand over her crop. Noon was only an hour away.

"Then I'll bring your wheat for you!" I announced.

"A-are you sure…?"

"Yes, leave it to me!"

"A-all right. Then please take this…"

She took a slip of paper out of her pocket and handed it to me. Written on it were the time and location of the delivery, along with the price of the wheat. It was a contract.

"Understood. Lia, Rose, I'll handle these, so you two please take Ms. Sandy to the infirmary!"

"Okay, that's fine, but…"

"Can you handle that by yourself, Allen?"

"Yeah, I'll be fine. Let's see… Once things settle down, let's meet by that big building over there."

I pointed to a nearby clock tower that you could easily spot from a distance.

"Sounds good," said Lia.

"Be careful," advised Rose.

"Thanks. Take care of Ms. Sandy," I replied.

After separating from them, I used the map drawn on the contract to find the delivery location.

"Here it is."

There was a store called *Rocky's Goods* at the spot the map indicated.

It would be a pain schlepping all this wheat into the store at once, so I'll just grab one sack for now.

I opened the rattly sliding door and walked inside with a bag of wheat. Soon, I found a man who looked like the store's owner.

"You a customer?" he asked.

"No, I'm a witchblade working for a farmer named Ms. Sandy. She hurt her back, so I'm delivering her harvest for her," I answered.

"...A witchblade, huh. Can I have a look at that document?"

"Yes, sir. Here you go."

I handed him the guaranty that Ms. Sandy had entrusted me with.

"Hmm..."

For some reason, he didn't even glance at the crop. Instead, he inspected me carefully from head to toe.

"I'll give you...half price."

"...Excuse me?"

"Did someone drop you on your head as a baby? I'm saying I'll buy the wheat for half the price that's stated on the contract."

"Huh?! Wh-why?!"

"It's pretty low-quality. You should be grateful I'm even giving you that much," he declared, picking a grain out of the bag.

"That's not true. This is very good wheat!"

"Come on, kid... What could a third-rate witchblade like you possibly know?"

"I can tell it's top-shelf at a glance. There are many farmers in my village, so I've seen a lot of wheat in my life. There's nothing wrong with this yield. I would even say that it's near perfect!"

The shopkeeper clicked his tongue loudly in blatant disgust.

"Tch, annoying brat... Excuse me, can you guys please do me a favor?" he called out.

Two large men emerged from the back of the store.

"Well, well, what do we have here? Some kind of trouble, Mr. Rocky?" one of the goons asked.

"Hmm, he looks like a swordsman...but he's just a kid," the other observed.

"Sorry to disturb you two for this. This brat won't listen to me, and I'm not sure what to do," the shopkeeper said.

The two men looked at each other and shrugged.

"What's wrong with you, short stuff? Kids aren't supposed to question their elders."

"You can still make up for this. Just say you're sorry to Mr. Rocky here, okay?"

They had to be bodyguards.

"...Mr. Rocky," I began.

"Heh-heh-heh, what is it?" he responded, giggling to himself.

"I don't understand why you would take issue with the quality of such great wheat and try to beat down the price. I ask you again: Please pay the proper amount."

He sighed loudly at my answer.

"Haah... This is why I've always hated witchblades. They're all a few cards short of a full deck. Sorry, guys, can you deal with him, please?"

"Ha-ha, guess we don't have a choice..."

"A little *education* is what unruly whelps like you need..."

Loosening their shoulders and necks, they approached me with long strides.

"Take this!"

One of the men drew back his right fist and then lunged toward me with a hook.

...What is he doing?

He shifted his body weight unnecessarily, his windup was pointlessly exaggerated, and even the way he clenched his fist was amateurish. His jab was nothing compared with Mr. Bonz's artful straight right.

"...Sorry about this."

I apologized, then delivered a backhand strike to his wide-open stomach.

"Hurggghhh?!"

He went pale from the impact, then fell flat on his face.

"Wh-what did you just do?!" the other bodyguard asked.

"...Huh? Did you not see it?" I responded.

I couldn't believe he would look away during a fight. They may have been big, but these two were clearly novices when it came to combat.

"Y-you'll pay for that!"

The remaining man raised his right hand and swung at me with a punch. His attempt was just as unpolished as the last bodyguard's.

"...Sorry."

"Ghah!"

I nailed him with a backhand in the exact same spot, knocking him unconscious immediately.

"Wh-what the hell...? You're no ordinary kid!"

The shopkeeper was visibly panicking after losing his two toughs in a matter of seconds. Now that they were out of the way, I could finally speak with him.

"Now, then..."

I took one step toward Mr. Rocky.

"Aiiieeeee!"

He yelped in fear, then fell on his back and scooted away from me.

"I would never make an unfair demand. I will ask this of you only *one more time*. Could you please pay the proper amount for this wheat?" I asked.

"Y-yes, of course! I'm sorry, I swear I'll never do this again! J-just spare my life, please!"

I never once claimed I was going to kill him...but whatever.

"Thank you. I'm going to bring in the crop. Where would you like me to leave the bags?"

"P-put them in front of the store, please! I'll carry them in later!"

"Thanks, I appreciate it."

I then unloaded all the bundles of wheat in the carriage and placed them in front of the store. Once I was finished, the shopkeeper thrust a leather purse bursting with cash toward me.

"Th-this is the full amount specified on the contract. Please count it yourself."

I checked the money just in case and confirmed it was the proper amount.

"Looks good. Have a nice day."

I gave a very slight bow, then spun around and started to leave.

"W-wait…just who are you?!" the man asked.

"No one important. As you said—I'm just a third-rate witchblade."

Now that I'd finished my delivery, I headed for the clock tower where Lia and Rose were waiting for me.

■

Once Allen broke off alone to head for Rocky's Goods, three people who'd been observing him from a considerable distance sprang to action.

"Hey, the target is alone! There's no longer any risk of injuring the princess!"

"Geez, finally. I'm already tired of this…"

"Let's off him quick and get outta here. We have other jobs waiting for us."

It was a trio of swordswomen who'd been hired to eliminate Allen. They made their living as assassins and dwelled permanently in the shadows. They were each rumored to be skilled enough with the blade to represent one of the Elite Five Academies.

"Roger that!"

"Geez, you don't have to say that every time… Why *wouldn't* we kill him quickly…?"

"Okay, let's move."

The women were hiding within a thick grove. They dropped down from a high tree in order to kill their target, but someone stopped them.

"Hmph, that's Reia for you. Her brain leaves a lot to be desired, but her instincts never let her down when it counts."

A man wearing a top hat and wielding a fancy black-and-white cane appeared in front of them. It was prisoner number 0018—Eighteen, the man whom Reia had tasked with protecting Allen.

"Who are you, geezer? Can you stop ogling at us like that? You're making me uncomfortable."

"Geez, what a pain... Let's just gut this creep..."

"There are no witnesses, and we're short on time... I guess we have no choice. Let's kill him."

Evidently, the three assassins didn't have any sort of moral code that would have prevented them from butchering people who weren't their targets. If someone stood in their way, they would remove them without hesitation.

Faced with their intense hostility, Eighteen studied the faces, figures, and outfits of the three swordswomen, then sighed loudly.

"Haah...you three don't understand a thing..."

They were all attractive in their own way. One of them had sharp, beautiful facial features, another looked innocent and youthful, and the last possessed dignity that almost reminded one of a fine sword. Their figures also left nothing to complain about, and their risqué clothing exposed a significant amount of skin.

Getting to see three such beautiful women would make any ordinary man's day.

Eighteen, however, was despondent. He wore the speechless expression of a man who had just clumsily toppled a long line of dominoes that he'd spent many painstaking years building up.

"Grovel—Coercion King!"

"Geez... Devour—Grand Eater!"

"Slumber in Ice—Permafrost!"

The menacing aura radiating from the three women would have been enough to make most faint, but Eighteen simply stood there and twirled his proud handlebar mustache.

"All three of you can use Soul Attire... You probably would have been a bit much for Allen. He doesn't yet have a full handle on his outsize strength," Eighteen admitted, cool as could be.

"I can't wait to hear how you cry!"

"Ha, can you at least go down cleanly? If you get blood on me, I'll kill you..."

"Let's make this quick and painless."

The three swordswomen brandished their Soul Attires and initiated a bloody struggle. It lasted less than a minute.

"Wh-what the...?"

"Geez... How...?"

"I-impossible..."

In the end, the women ended up on their hands and knees, unable to stand. One blow apiece had shattered each of their Soul Attires and rendered their minds hazy. Eighteen, on the other hand, didn't have a scratch on him and hadn't broken a sweat.

The difference in strength was astounding.

"You all have such wonderful gifts, yet you truly understand nothing."

He directed his harsh glare at the outfits of the women.

"Those awful clothes were designed to invite the looks of men. How deplorable... What a waste."

Eighteen continued to leisurely proselytize.

"I won't blame you for being conscious of the eyes of others. It's only right for men and women of class to look after their appearance. However! Normalizing the feeling of being stared at causes one to lose their shame...and once that happens, it's all over."

He shook his head, sadness visible in his eyes.

"You three have gotten drunk off of being stared at and have elected to intentionally *show* your bodies to the world... As a result, you now *depend* on the gaze of others."

Eighteen raised his voice to bring his argument to a close.

"Nothing beats the natural behavior of a girl who doesn't realize she's being peeped on! Her expressionless face, her little idiosyncrasies, and the ultimate embarrassment when she realizes someone is watching her—these elements all come together in perfect harmony to create true beauty!"

He looked down at their clothes one last time.

Their tops accentuated their chests, their skirts were so short that it didn't take much to see under them, and their stomachs were bare. The outfits ran contrary to his sense of beauty in every way.

"You three chose to expose yourselves and lost your shame in the process. You aren't even worth peeping in on."

Now finished waxing poetic about his aesthetic theory, he contacted his mistress, Reia, and gave her a detailed report of the incident.

■

After successfully delivering the wheat, I headed for the clock tower where we'd decided to meet up. When I arrived, I found Rose standing there alone, staring into space.

"Hey, Rose. How is Ms. Sandy doing?"

"It was chronic back pain. The doctor said she'll be fine after a little rest."

"That's good to hear."

I was glad it didn't seem to be a major injury.

"Where's Lia?"

"She's still at the hospital. She said she couldn't leave Ms. Sandy alone in that state, so she stayed to keep her company."

"That sounds like her."

Her consideration for others was one of her greatest virtues.

We decided to join back up with Lia and Ms. Sandy. The infirmary was only a three-minute walk from the clock tower. After checking in at the reception area, we walked to Ms. Sandy's room.

"We're back. How are you feeling, Ms. Sandy?" I asked.

"Oh, it's Allen. Sorry for all the trouble I've caused you…but I'm fine now, thanks to your help. I'm truly grateful," she answered.

"Don't worry about it. Here's the money from the wheat delivery."

I pulled the small leather pouch out of my pocket and handed it to her.

"Oh dear, I owe you three so much."

"Just think of this as a continuation of our escort duty."

That was a wrap on this job.

"Thank you, Lia," I whispered in her ear.

"No problem. This was nothing," she responded with a kind smile.

Just as I was about to suggest we leave, Ms. Sandy spoke up.

"By the way, what are you three planning on doing after this? Since you arrived in Drestia today, how about enjoying the annual Unity Festival?" she suggested.

"That was actually next on our list," I answered.

"Oh, wonderful! I recommend renting some *yukata*! It wouldn't do to go to a festival wearing your school uniforms," she insisted, smiling.

"What's a *yukata*?" Lia asked, confused.

"It's a traditional kind of clothing in this country," explained Rose.

Lia had apparently never heard of them while living in Vesteria.

"That could be fun!" she said.

"Those uniforms would stand out a little too much. I think it's a great idea," added Ms. Sandy.

It was certainly true that *yukata* would draw less attention than uniforms from the famous Thousand Blade Academy.

"Yeah... It's not every day you get to go to a festival. We should do it," I agreed.

"There's a nice store right in front of this hospital called Yukata Rental! It's been there since I was a young girl. All the employees are very kind!" Ms. Sandy informed us.

"That sounds great. We should check it out," I responded.

It felt much better going to a store someone had suggested to you than going to one you had never heard of.

"All right, it's time we head out. I hope we see each other again, Ms. Sandy," I said.

"I hope your back gets better soon!" Lia exclaimed.

"Good luck with your recovery," added Rose.

"Thank you. Take care of yourselves," responded Ms. Sandy.

We left the hospital and quickly found the *yukata*-rental store the old woman had recommended.

"Wanna go in?" I asked.

"Yeah, let's do it!" responded Lia.

"I wonder how long it's been since I last wore a *yukata*...," murmured Rose.

We entered without much thought.

"Welcome. Are you looking to rent some *yukata*?"

A gentle-mannered old lady wearing a vibrant summer kimono approached us.

"Yes, we would like three of them," I answered.

"Great, you've come to the right place!" she said.

The lady then raised her voice and called deeper into the store.

"Hey, we have a male customer! Someone come out and help!"

I heard hurried footsteps, and a male employee in a *yukata* emerged.

"Welcome to our store! Let's see... We have our male offerings over here. Please come with me," he urged.

I followed him to the end of the store.

"Please select the outfit you like best."

Lined up in front of me was a collection of men's rental kimonos. Unsurprisingly, there weren't as many as there were for women, but there were still enough that settling on one was difficult. I took a brief look at all of them, then arrived at a decision.

"I would like this one, please."

I picked out a plain black one so I wouldn't stand out too much.

"All right... There we go. Now, if you'll follow me, I'll help you put it on."

"Thank you."

He guided me into the men's changing room. It only took me less than a minute to put my outfit on and tie a white sash around it. Men tend to get dressed quickly.

"This looks very nice on you!"

I saw the reflection of myself in my *yukata* in the mirror in front of me. It made me feel a little awkward.

"Th-thank you very much..."

I left the changing room and waited for Lia and Rose. Ten minutes later, the door to the women's changing room opened.

"H-how do I look...?" asked Lia.

"Do you think this suits me?" asked Rose.

They both emerged in elegant summer kimonos—a huge change of pace from the school uniforms I was used to seeing them in.

"…"

My breath caught in my throat. Their beauty left me at a loss for words.

Lia was wearing a thin, tan kimono decorated with crimson dragonflies. Her sash was the same dark red as the ribbons that held her pigtails.

Rose's navy-blue outfit was adorned with white cherry blossom petals, and her sash was embroidered with yellow thread.

It wasn't flattery to say the two were stunning in their *yukata*.

"Y-yes, they both look great on you," I stammered.

"R-really? Thank you," Lia muttered, blushing.

"Ha, I'm glad you like it," Rose said with a happy smile.

"Y-yours looks very good on you, too, Allen."

"The calm color suits you."

"Ah-ha-ha, thanks."

After sharing our thoughts on our *yukata*, we paid for the rentals and finally headed for the Unity Festival.

■

There was a road in the center of Drestia called Holy Street, where the largest festival in Liengard, the Unity Festival, was held once a year. Lia, Rose, and I were currently walking down it.

"I didn't realize just how many folks there were here until now…," I remarked.

"Yeah, this is way more people than I've ever seen in Aurest. It's rare to see a crowd this large even in Vesteria," claimed Lia.

"That's Drestia for you," said Rose.

They both nodded in agreement.

The sea of figures around us extended in all directions. Closely packed street stalls lined both sides of the street, and the employees at each stand called out in lively voices to attract customers. The scent of food stimulated my appetite. I'd never seen a grander festival.

We continued down the crowded street until Lia and Rose saw something that caught their interest.

"Look, Allen! Chocolate bananas!"

"There are candy apples over there!"

They pointed in different directions.

"Ah-ha-ha, nice. Can you both get me one?" I asked.

"Yeah!"

"Sure!"

We spent some time going to a variety of stalls and sampling many dishes. We started with the chocolate bananas and the candy apples, then moved on to grilled squid, *yakisoba*, fried chicken, cotton candy, and sausages on sticks... My stomach already felt like it was going to burst.

One person in particular was at fault for why we stopped at so many food stalls—Lia. Her stomach was truly bottomless. In fact, she ate so much that it made me want to ask where in her body she stored all that grub.

It's not like I can say that to a girl, though...

Problem was, I didn't know how else to stop her unending rampage of gluttony.

"Wow, check that out, Allen! That stall has beef-sirloin kebabs! They look amazing!"

Lia's eyes sparkled as she pointed at a new stall. It was selling beef sirloin lathered in thick grease.

Urgh...

I had no idea how I was going to cram that in given how stuffed I already was. I felt like I was getting heartburn just glancing at it.

I picked up on this a little when we ate ramzacs, but Lia can pack in a fearsome amount. Calling her a big eater might even be underselling her.

If she could eat that much and maintain her healthy frame, I wasn't going to comment. But I wanted no part in trying to keep up with her appetite.

Rose and I glanced at each other and nodded.

"H-hey, Lia. Aren't you getting a little full?" I asked.

"I think we've already had a good amount…," added Rose.

"Huh, what are you guys saying? We're just getting started!" Lia exclaimed, patting me on the back.

She has room for more?!

I needed to give serious thought to what I should do when I dined with her in the future.

I might explode if I eat anything else…

Somehow, I needed to get her mind off food.

"How about we check out some other kinds of stalls? There's plenty more to do here besides chow down," I suggested.

"Ooh, that's a good idea! I second that!" added Rose, jumping on my proposal.

"Okay…if that's what you both want, then sure!" Lia agreed cheerfully. She ended up not resisting.

Rose and I breathed a sigh of relief at being freed from the torturous food-stand gauntlet.

Then we walked around the festival and hit up a variety of game stalls. We tried out a lottery, goldfish scooping, ring toss, and more. Lia's accuracy was godlike—she won countless prizes, including stuffed animals, figures, and button pins. Rose, meanwhile, was astoundingly good at the super ball–scooping game.

They both ended up with a large collection of spoils.

"Whooo! We scored big!"

"Hmm-hmm, those games were no match for us!"

Satisfied, they hoisted their prizes high in the air.

"Ah-ha-ha…the stall workers looked ready to cry…," I remarked.

We continued to amble around and enjoy the Unity Festival.

…Hmm? What's that?

I spotted a building in front of us with heavy security.

It's huge. Is that seven floors?

A great number of swordfighters were standing around the edifice. Their lack of uniforms signified that they probably weren't holy knights.

What in the world is this thing for?

I stared absentmindedly at the structure and the large crowd guarding it.

"That's the Unity Trade Center. The Five Business Oligarchs are probably holding a conference there right now," Rose explained, noticing I was staring at it.

The *Five Business Oligarchs*—that was a nickname used to refer to five incredibly wealthy merchants who held as much influence in Liengard as the chairs of the Elite Five Academies. The people outside the building probably belonged to their private armies.

"You know everything, Rose," I complimented.

"No, I don't. My grandfather just brought me here once, so I learned a little about this city then," she explained.

"Your grandfather... Is he the one who taught you the Cherry Blossom—?"

Suddenly, a massive explosion in the Unity Trade Center cut me off.

"HUH?!"

Immediately afterward, groups of people wearing hooded black overcoats streamed out of the nearby buildings and rushed into the Trade Center. They were unfazed, as if they'd known the explosion would be happening, and their cloaks obscured their faces. It was clear they were the criminals behind this incident.

They must be after the business oligarchs.

While I took time to gather my thoughts, the area around us fell into total chaos.

"Th-the Trade Center is on fire!"

"Oh my god, someone call the holy knights!"

"Hurry! The Five Business Oligarchs are in there!"

Some of the private soldiers cried out for the holy knights, some silently rushed into the building, and some stood frozen in place. Despite being placed in charge of security, they were totally disorganized.

The fire from the explosion actually isn't that bad.

Additionally, the building's exterior appeared to be made of concrete—which meant the blaze would travel slowly. The holy knights would be able to extinguish the flames as soon as they arrived.

With that in mind, what I needed to do was use my skills as a swordsman to help anyone in immediate need.

"I'm going in. Wait here, you two!"

"I-I'm going in, too!"

"I'm coming with you!"

The three of us then rushed into the smoldering Unity Trade Center.

■

Within the structure, a fierce battle was unfolding.

"*Blargh!*"

"*Gaaah!*"

The private soldiers who'd charged into the building without hesitation were quite skilled. They used flashy swordcraft to cut down an entire group of black-garbed criminals, then rushed up the staircase. Based on how they prioritized getting upstairs, the Five Business Oligarchs had to be on the top floor of the seven-story edifice.

"Lia, Rose, let's follow them!"

We trailed behind the dependable private soldiers as they ascended, but then we stopped dead in our tracks at the sixth floor.

"*Gah...*"

"I-impossible!"

"How...can he...?"

A lone, black-garbed swordsman had cut down every last private soldier.

"...Weak, weak, weak! How can your whole crew possibly be this pathetic?! Is this really all the fun you can give me? Ah-ha, ah-ha-ha, ah-ha-ha-ha-ha-ha!"

He stomped on the collapsed private soldiers and laughed unsettlingly.

...This guy is bad news.

I readied myself and reached for the sword at my hip.

"Oh my god... Omigod, omigod, omigod, omigod, omigod, omigod... Is that really you, Allen?!"

"...?!"

I could see him sneering under his hood, and his voice sounded full of joy as he called my name.

"Ha-ha, it *is* you! I would never mistake you! Ah-ha… Oh, how long I've waited to see you again!"

He clapped his hands as his shoulders shook happily.

"…Who are you?" I asked.

I was sure I would have remembered meeting someone this unhinged.

"Ah-ha, you're so cruel… How could you have forgotten the violent love we shared for each other?"

I had no idea what he was going on about. One thing was clear, though—he was infatuated with me.

I have no choice here, do I…?

I steeled myself for combat.

"Allen, go ahead of us and find the Five Business Oligarchs!" urged Lia.

"We'll handle him," announced Rose.

They both drew their blades emphatically and stepped in front of me.

"This guy will be nothing against the two of us together!"

"Leave him to us!"

"…Got it."

They were confident they could handle him, so I decided to trust them. Leaving them there, I rushed up to the seventh floor, where the business oligarchs were.

"Huh?! Allen, don't abandon me!" the swordsman called after me, sounding as though he was going to cry.

"Look this way!"

"You have to deal with us first!"

I heard the harsh *clang* of blade meeting blade.

■

I dashed up the stairs, opened a door with VIP ROOM written on it, and raced inside.

"E-eeeeeek!"

"P-please spare my life!"

"I-I-I'll give you money! I'll buy you whatever you want!"

Three people who had to be business oligarchs cried out successively in trembling voices. They were probably mistaking me for a criminal. I supposed I couldn't blame them for being afraid.

The other two have nerves of steel...

The first of this pair was a one-eyed man with a large scar over his left eye. The other was a beautiful woman with slanted, fox-like eyes and red hair. I felt as if I'd seen her somewhere before, but now wasn't the time to dig through my memory. Our lives could be at risk if I didn't gain their trust and get them out of here fast.

"I'm a witchblade named Allen Rodol. I'm here to save you all," I announced.

The terror in their eyes faded. Naturally, however, they didn't trust me entirely yet. For that reason, I decided to inform them of a potential threat that would frighten them into hightailing it out of here.

"As you're aware, a bomb was planted in this building. We have no guarantee that it was the only one. There's a chance that there's a much larger explosive somewhere...and I would bet that it's close by."

That mysterious band of villains had been able to set a bomb in this building without anyone noticing.

They would have no problem leveling this entire edifice if they felt like it. But instead, they opted for an explosive of only moderate strength.

Going off that, it was clear that their goal wasn't to kill the Five Business Oligarchs—it was to kidnap them. These five far surpassed the chairs of the Elite Five Academies in terms of financial power, so the criminals would be able to ask for enormous ransoms in return for their release.

Even if the goal is abduction, however, that doesn't mean the lives of the business oligarchs aren't in danger.

It wasn't hard to imagine that the criminals would just kill these five the moment that capturing them failed. There was a high chance they'd set a bomb near the VIP room for that scenario.

Which was why we needed to flee from this place quickly.

"I—I—I see!"

"L-let's l-leave straight away!"

"Allen, was it? C-can you take us out of here?!"

As I'd expected, the Five Business Oligarchs were quick on the uptake. Even amid the panic of this violent, unfamiliar situation, they could still make the right call.

"Of course. Follow me!"

I led them out of the VIP room, aiming to hurry them out of the Unity Trade Center as soon as possible. We dashed down the stairs, but when we reached the sixth floor, I was met with a startling sight: Lia lying on her back, totally still.

"...L-Lia?"

I rushed over to her and put my hand to her chest.

Thank goodness...

Her heart was beating healthily. She was just unconscious. I felt relieved, then looked around.

"Cherry Blossom Blade Secret Technique—Mirror Sakura Slash!"

"Ah-ha...that toy won't work against me!"

"What the...? AHHH!"

The man easily dodged Rose's powerful attack, then struck her with a fierce frontal kick, sending her flying backward.

"Rose!"

The back of her head crashed into the concrete wall behind her, and she fell to the floor, motionless. She had been knocked unconscious.

He defeated Lia and Rose...

There was no way they both could have lost to this eccentric swordsman in a fair fight.

Something must have given him the edge he needed to bring them down...

This man must have had some fearsome power that tripped them up.

"Haah..."

I exhaled to calm the rage that was beginning to boil in my head and heart. Taking a second to examine my surroundings, I saw some private soldiers who were holding their weapons in trembling hands.

"I'll take care of him. You all escort the Five Business Oligarchs outside," I commanded.

"A-are you sure?!"

"O-okay!"

"We'll leave him to you!"

I nodded, and the private soldiers took the oligarchs and ran. My foe didn't even try to stop them; he simply stared at me.

"…I thought you would have cut them off," I said.

"Ah-haaa! *You're* so much more important to me than some deathly boring orders!"

He wasn't kidding; he really was only interested in me.

"Who *are* you?" I asked.

The black hood over his head prevented me from making out his face.

"Oof, I'm offended that you would forget me…because not a day or night has gone by that I haven't thought of you, Allen," he yelled, throwing his arms wide and laughing.

"We don't have much time here. Wanna go ahead and reveal yourself?"

There was still a high likelihood there were more bombs set in this building, so I didn't want to be here any longer than I had to be.

"There's no need to rush things. You'll spoil our special reunion… *Reject Swordsman*."

"…?!"

Reject Swordsman. The only people who knew that nickname were students from Grand Swordcraft Academy—my middle school.

Who from there could be this obsessed with me…?

Only a single individual sprang to mind.

"Don't tell me…is that you, Dodriel?!"

"Ah-haaa! Bingo, correctamundo! Salutations, Allen, my old friend!" he shouted, throwing back his hood.

Although his tied-back blue hair was terribly damaged, he was still handsome. But the most striking feature of his complexion was the large scar on his forehead. I'd given him that during our duel.

"Dodriel Barton…"

"Ah-haaa… You finally remembered me, Allen Rodoooool!"

The way he called my name made my hair stand on end.

"Why haven't you gotten rid of that gash?" I asked, pointing at the gruesome shape on his forehead.

Medical science in Liengard was very advanced. A scar of that size should have been easy to remove.

"You dummy, I couldn't dream of giving it up it… It's the physical proof of our love, after all!"

Dodriel stroked the scar affectionately.

"After *that day*, I ruminated ceaselessly about how I, a prodigy, could have possibly lost to the Reject Swordsman. I racked my brain for what I'd done wrong, but I could never come up with an answer. Instead, I toiled in never-ending pain and regret, crying every day…"

He flicked his eyes at me, then continued:

"I opted to keep this hideous visage so that I would never forget my pain, my grudge. Every time I woke up and saw it in the mirror, I would seethe with hatred for you. That resentment ended up inspiring me to put forth *effort* for the first time in my entire life! I practiced my swordcraft day after day, dawn until dusk! All with the goal of killing you!"

He looked totally twisted by insanity. But the next moment, he seemed to undergo a sudden personality shift and smiled peacefully.

"However…as I spent my days ruled by my loathing for you and my desire for vengeance, I came to a sudden realization—that you love me, Allen."

…What in the world is he talking about?

"And that was when I came to love you, too… Actually, it's possible that the dormant feelings of affection I'd always possessed simply exploded to the surface. You took up permanent residence in my mind, my heart, and my soul! I never stopped thinking of you, and before I knew it, I was head over heels!"

His speech was completely incoherent; he must have been totally broken.

"You're obviously not going to give me a normal conversation," I remarked.

"Ah-haaa, you're right about that! How could I possibly be normal around you? Let's give ourselves over to passion!"

Dodriel thrust the tip of his blade before me, and I responded by assuming the middle stance. But as we stood facing each other, I realized something.

"That's Soul Attire, isn't it?"

I sensed an uncanny aura rising from his weapon. Something about it set it apart from any old sword you could get off the street.

"Well spotted! It's very plain, but this is indeed my Soul Attire. You know me so well!"

As his face glowed with ecstasy, he wrapped his arms around his body and squirmed. I ignored his eccentric behavior and calmly considered the situation.

I can't believe he manifested his Soul Attire in such a short period of time...

Creepy as he was, Dodriel was a true prodigy.

I can't even begin to guess what kind of power it houses from its appearance.

Lia's Fafnir was covered in flames, and Shido's Vanargand released cold air, so I'd been able to gauge their abilities pretty accurately.

But nothing stood out about Dodriel's weapon—not on the blade, and not on the grip. Aura aside, it really just looked like an ordinary sword you could find anywhere.

The best thing to do in this situation is attack right away!

I couldn't afford to let him strike first. The most optimal way forward was defeating him before he would be able to use his Soul Attire's power. And even if I couldn't pull that off, getting him to expose his Soul Attire's defensive capabilities would be advantageous at the very least. By contrast, allowing him to unleash his unknown offensive powers against me would be the worst-case scenario—if my reaction was even a second off, the results could be fatal.

"Let's do this, Dodriel."

"Ah-haaa...don't worry, Allen! I'm not going anywhere!"

Dodriel opened his arms wide and smiled unsettlingly. He wasn't adopting any kind of stance; he'd left himself literally defenseless.

I see he's still just as careless and conceited as ever. He may be a prodigy, but that self-assurance is one of his few real weaknesses!

I took a step forward to approach him.

"Eighth Style—Eight-Span Crow!"

Then I released eight sharp slash attacks at once, aiming for his arms, legs, neck, torso, and chest—but he didn't so much as budge.

...Is he giving up?

That thought was quickly driven out of my mind when all eight of the slash attacks passed through his body.

"Huh?!"

"Ah-haaa, how do you explain that?"

He ignored my astonishment and took a large step forward.

"Autumn Rain Style—Rainy Season!"

Dodriel proceeded to unleash one malicious thrust after another.

"Wha—?!"

I leaped back far, somehow avoiding blows to my vital points.

He got my right shoulder and my left flank...

Fortunately, the wounds were light. The dull pain would limit my movement, but I was sure I could still keep fighting.

Damn, he's way faster than he used to be...

Dodriel had clearly done more than just gain Soul Attire. His physical capabilities and his swordcraft had both improved to an astonishing degree.

"Oh, come on, don't be a scaredy-cat," he mocked, shrugging and snickering.

"What the heck did you just do?" I asked.

I knew my Eight-Span Crow should have hit him. But somehow, all eight slices had passed *through* his body.

There's no defensive technique that can explain that.

Instead, he'd almost certainly harnessed the power of his Soul Attire. He must have utilized this strange technique to defeat Lia and Rose.

"Ah-haaa! It truly is an enigma, isn't it?"

Zigzagging to left and right, Dodriel closed the distance between us in an instant. His erratic movement made it difficult to tell how far he was from me.

"Autumn Rain Secret Technique—Downpour!"

He performed a sharp central thrust.

I can dodge this!

In terms of simple swordcraft skill, Rose far surpassed him.

"Too slow!"

I swiped my blade up from the bottom right to force away his assault, breaking his posture. Then I followed up with the trickiest move to evade in my arsenal.

"Cherry Blossom Blade Secret Technique—Mirror Sakura Slash!"

Eight lightning-quick slash attacks, four from the left and four from the right, closed in on Dodriel.

I will see his Soul Attire's power this time!

I opened my eyes wide and analyzed his every action.

...Huh?

The next moment, he did something quite peculiar—he took a step forward. Didn't dodge the attack, didn't guard with his blade—he simply took a step forward. That meant this specific movement was the best choice over attempting to dodge or defend himself.

My eight slash attacks then passed through his body.

"Ah-haaa! I wonder why you can't hit me? Autumn Rain Style—Torrential Rain!"

He unleashed a deluge of counterattacks, including downward

diagonal slashes, downward vertical slashes, upward vertical slashes, and thrusts.

"Wha—?!"

Despite working as hard as I could to defend myself, dodging all his slashes from point-blank range proved difficult, so I ended up suffering a few wounds.

That's okay. I figured out his secret!

He'd stepped forward to stand on a very specific spot—within my shadow. When my slashes had approached him, he'd lunged into my shadow without hesitation. That evidence brought me to one conclusion.

"Your Soul Attire gives you the ability to hide in shadows, doesn't it?"

As long as he was standing in his opponent's silhouette, he could render all their strikes ineffective.

"Right on the money again! You're good at this! You're the first person to figure out the secret of my Shadow Sovereign! We don't even need words to understand each other... You and I really are bound by the red thread of fate!"

Dodriel paused, his face twisting with happiness.

"But, Allen, my dear, do you really think you can accomplish anything with that knowledge? Look around. Losing your shadow isn't going to be easy."

He directed his gaze exaggeratedly around the room. On top of the numerous fluorescent lights that were built into the ceiling, sunlight also shone in through the building's broken windows. With this many light sources, it would be impossible to avoid casting a shadow.

"...I still have some moves up my sleeve."

"Oh-ho, now that's interesting. I can't wait to see them!"

As soon as he finished his spiel, Dodriel rushed directly at me. I held my middle stance, coolly gathering my thoughts.

There's one thing I know for a fact—there's nothing in this world I can't cut.

If a swordfighter ever comes across something they can't cut through, then that's only due to a limitation of their skill. As someone who'd torn through the very fabric of another world, I knew that better than anyone.

That's right. I'd be wrong to believe I can't rend him with my blade.

I calmly played back our previous interaction in my mind.

My slices back then passed through him without leaving a single scratch... That means that when he steps into my shadow, his true body *leaves this world and enters what I'll call the Shadow World.*

If my theory was correct, then the solution to my conundrum was simple: I just needed to tear that space to shreds, just like I'd done with the World of Time!

"It was nice knowing you, Allen! Autumn Rain Secret Technique—Downpour!"

Dodriel stepped into my shadow and unleashed a sharp thrust that was aimed for my heart. But I had my response at the ready.

"Fifth Style—World Render!"

"Huhhhh?!"

My strongest technique, so powerful that it had destroyed the World of Time, cut through both his Downpour and the Shadow World in one fell swoop.

"Ah-ha-haaa... I-incredible. That's why I love you, Allen..."

He praised me meekly as blood flowed from his chest.

"You fought well, too."

Dodriel had barely avoided a lethal blow by making a split-second decision to jump back from my attack. The injury he'd sustained wasn't shallow, though, so it would be unwise for him to continue fighting.

In the distance, the black-garbed criminals who'd been watching us started to speak.

"D-did he really just...?!"

"He beat the rookie?!"

"R-retreat!"

They fled as soon as they saw that I'd bested Dodriel.

"Ah-ha... May we meet again...," he uttered in parting, before

jumping out of the window behind him and disappearing with the
rest of his compatriots.

■

I wasn't able to stop the criminals from escaping after I defeated
Dodriel. I simply didn't have the time.

"Lia, Rose…get up!"

I shook them hard by the shoulders but got no response from
either one.

"Dammit…"

After picking them up in each arm, I sprinted for the building's
entrance.

Please tell me I'm just overthinking things…

The criminals had briskly exited the structure. Way too quick. The
convenient timing of their retreat frightened me.

I couldn't stop thinking about the possibility of a second, much
larger explosive.

"Aaaaaaaahhhh!"

I flew down the stairs with my downward momentum, descending
from the sixth floor to the fifth floor, the fifth floor to the fourth floor,
the fourth floor to the third floor—all while being careful not to jostle
the unconscious girls too much.

"Almost there!"

When I finally reached the ground floor and caught sight of the exit,
I heard a *click*.

No!!!!

The next moment, a large eruption that dwarfed the previous one
burst forth. It had likely originated from the VIP room on the seventh
floor. The explosion was far stronger than I expected—it was powerful
enough to level not just this building, but also the entire area surrounding it as well.

"Aaaaaaahhhhhhhhhh!"

I booked it as fast as I could. No matter my training, however, I was
only human. Outrunning an explosion was simply impossible.

Crap, I'm not gonna make it…

In a last-ditch effort to save them, I enveloped the unconscious Lia and Rose with my body.

If I can at least shield them a little from the blast…!

Holding hope in my heart, I waited for the impact.

"Desiccate—Withered Umbrella!"

The blast vanished right before it was about to hit us.

"…Huh?"

This sudden turn of events left me dumbstruck.

"This explosion would hae been nothing without the element of surprise," called the red-haired woman who'd caused it to disappear. She laughed bewitchingly.

"Wh-who are…?" I began, but I was quickly interrupted.

"You're the best, Lady Rize!"

"That was amazing! That's the lone woman of the Five Business Oligarchs for you!"

"House Dorhein is in great hands!"

The people around us cheered for her.

Did they say "House Dorhein"?

She had the same last name as Ferris Dorhein, the chairwoman of Ice King Academy. Upon closer inspection, her facial features and clothes resembled Ferris's as well.

The woman had smooth, supple skin and slanted, fox-like eyes. She was wearing a beautiful red-and-white kimono that blazed like fire. Her long red hair was tied into an elegant side bun, and she had donned an ornate hairpin that was modeled after a flame.

I wonder if they're sisters, I thought.

"U-urgh…"

"Wh-where am I?"

Lia and Rose had regained consciousness.

"Lia, Rose! You're awake!"

I was relieved to see they were okay.

"Allen…? O-oh yeah, where is he?!"

"What happened to that swordsman?!"

They probably meant Dodriel. After rising to their feet, they surveyed their surroundings.

"Don't worry. I defeated him."

"R-really...? Guess I shouldn't be surprised..."

"...Damn."

Lia and Rose each chewed their bottom lip in silence. They were clearly unhappy about having lost to him.

What should I say at a time like this...?

While I was pondering that, someone suddenly addressed me.

"Thank you, young Allen. Ye saved me."

It was the woman from the famed House Dorhein, whom the bystanders had showered with praise after she'd banished the explosion. Her northern accent was a little stronger than Ferris's.

"No, you're the one who saved us. What you did was incredible... I can't believe you made a blast that huge just disappear," I answered.

I was sure I'd heard her call out "Withered Umbrella." I wondered what her Soul Attire was capable of.

"No, that was just a li'l self-defense technique. Ye're such a flatterer, Allen," she said jokingly, hiding her mouth with her kimono sleeve and giggling.

"H-huh..."

The brief aura I'd felt a few moments ago had definitely exceeded that of a simple self-defense technique. She was obviously humble about her strength.

"Oops, I havenae introduced myself. I'm Rize Dorhein, one of the so-called Five Business Oligarchs, and I run a modest company called Fox Financing. It's very nice to meet ye," she greeted.

"My name is Allen Rodol. I'm a student of Thousand Blade Academy, but due to certain circumstances, I'm currently working as a witchblade," I explained.

"Aha, I knew it was you!" Rize exclaimed, clapping her hands together and nodding.

"You know who I am...?"

"My little sister, Ferris, has told me a little about you."

"Oh, I see."

As I'd suspected, Rize and Ferris were sisters.

"I heard ye defeated her favorite pup, Shido. She told me she was going tae get ye for that. Blew her top, she did."

"U-um, well…"

"Hee-hee, don't worry about it. Ferris just has a wee bit of a temper," consoled Rize, waving her hands back and forth.

In stark contrast to the slightly…unfortunate dispositions of Chairwoman Reia and Ferris, Rize projected an elegant, mature aura.

"Hmm, I really owe ye one now… How can I repay you?" she asked, frowning in thought.

"Y-you don't need to repay me. I only did what was expected of me as a swordsman—," I began, trying to politely refuse.

"That willnae do. It is my belief that *one should always repay their debts*. I willnae feel right until I return the favor," Rize interrupted, placing a thin index finger on my lips. "Let's see… How about this? Next time ye find yerself in a great amount of trouble, come find me. Just once, I will grant ye my strength for anything you may need."

"A-anything?"

"Yes, that's right. Anything."

I'd been given the opportunity to ask a member of the Five Business Oligarchs to assist me for whatever I wanted.

This is an enormous privilege I've just received…

The Five Business Oligarchs held as much sway in Liengard as the chairs of the Elite Five Academies. Even if it was only a onetime thing, being able to call on her help was a tremendous card to have up my sleeve.

Rize then leaned forward to whisper into my ear.

"I'm not my little sister. I find you quite fascinating."

"…! I'm flattered that you would think anything of someone like me… I don't know what to say!"

It made me very happy to know that a swordswoman who yielded such an incredible Soul Attire had taken a shine to me.

...Oh yeah. I can use her offer to ask her to train with me. That's a great idea!

I didn't need much money, and I didn't have much want for material things. As long I had the bare amount of funds to live a comfortable life with Mom, I would be fine.

"Oh, I just love yer rustic simplicity..." Rize sighed, dragging me away from my thoughts. For some reason, she was licking her lips with a spellbound expression.

"Excuse me, you're clearly bothering Allen..."

"Can you please back off?"

Lia and Rose stepped between me and her, each making a stern expression.

"I see you two are quite protective of him," Rize said, snickering as she took a step back.

Our friendly conversation now brought to a halt, she narrowed her fox-like eyes and gave us a warning.

"I don't mean tae scare ye with this, but you three should think more of yer safety from now on. Those black-garbed nasties belong to the Black Organization, which has been causing so much trouble in society as of late."

"...I suspected as much," I responded.

That possibility had occurred to me because of their distinctive clothes, but I couldn't believe it was actually them.

The Black Organization was a large-scale criminal group that had been wreaking havoc in this country in recent years. They took part in a great variety of offenses, including the manufacturing and smuggling of drugs, human trafficking, and the assassination of major figures. And now I knew Dodriel was a member.

I'd wanted to avoid getting involved with them.

This time, however, I had no choice. A mysterious group had appeared out of nowhere and had started attacking defenseless civilians. If I'd decided not to act, I would have regretted it for the rest of my life.

I made what was objectively the right call.

"Thank you for the warning," I added.

"Ye're welcome. Okay, I have some cleaning up tae do, so I will take my leave of ye here. May we meet again, Allen," Rize announced.

"Yes, I look forward to it," I responded.

After parting ways with her, the three of us returned to the rental store to pay for our ruined *yukata*. Word of the incident had reached the shop, however, so the employees thanked us on behalf of Drestia and told us we didn't need to reimburse them.

■

It had been exactly three weeks since the turmoil of the Unity Festival.

After completing every job Mr. Bonz selected for us today—slaying a giant worm, collecting around three kilograms of rare grass, and putting down a goblin lord—we delivered our report at the Witch-blade Guild's reception area.

"Thanks for your hard work over the last month, Allen, Lia, and Rose!"

Mr. Bonz went out of his way to leave the reception desk and give us each a firm handshake. Since it had been exactly one month since we'd been suspended from the academy, this was our final day as witchblades.

"Thank you for everything, Mr. Bonz," I said.

"Thank you very much!" exclaimed Lia.

"It's been fun," added Rose.

"Ha, no need for thanks! You kids helped me a ton with cleaning up the request backlog!" Mr. Bonz answered.

We finished saying our good-byes to him, and a crowd of people approached us.

"Allen...I'm gonna miss you, man..."

"Haah, it's gonna be so depressing without Lady Lia and Lady Rose around to brighten up the place..."

"Come here to hang out any time! We'll always be open after class."

Dred and the other witchblades were sorry to see us go. Although they behaved and spoke like ruffians, they were all decent once you got to know them.

"Thank you so much for helping us out over the last month!" I responded.

"Thank you for everything. Please say hi if you ever spot me in the city!" said Lia.

"I hope to see you all again soon," added Rose.

After we said our farewells to everyone, we left the Witchblade Guild. It was already dim outside, and the cool air calmed my body and mind.

"That sure was an eventful month, but the assignments were enjoyable," I reflected aloud.

"Yeah, it was one surprise after another at first, but now we can look back on all of it and laugh," agreed Lia.

"Being a witchblade is dangerous, but it's engaging work," concurred Rose.

I had always liked the idea of becoming a holy knight and earning a steady salary as I worked for the safety of society. After this last month, however, my worldview had expanded. I felt like becoming a witchblade and helping people by taking on their requests wouldn't be such a bad life.

"Okay...it's already late, so do you want to split up now?" I asked.

"Yeah, sure. We're finally returning to Thousand Blade Academy tomorrow!" Lia proclaimed.

"We can finally start Soul Attire Acquisition class then, too. I'm looking forward to it," said Rose.

And thus, after getting through our month as witchblades, we returned to school at Thousand Blade Academy.

CHAPTER 2

Conflict at School

After completing our suspension by finishing our one-month training stint as witchblades, Lia, Rose, and I gathered in front of the chairwoman's office. I knocked on the entrance just as I always did and opened the door after being given permission to enter.

"Excuse us," I said.

Chairwoman Reia was there, looking as healthy as ever, as well as Eighteen, who looked more dejected than I'd ever seen him. She must have worked him especially hard over the last month.

"Hey, you're back! ...Very nice. I can tell that you three have gotten tougher from the expressions on your faces," she said, inspecting us closely.

"Ah-ha-ha, we went through quite a lot...," I responded.

"We sure had our share of incidents," added Lia.

"It was an action-packed month," said Rose.

Looking back, we really did go through a lot in a small amount of time. It might have been more accurate to say my countenance had become *older* rather than *tougher*.

"Wonderful. I'd like you to tell me about everything you went through someday," the chairwoman expressed with a smile. "But for now, I'll lift your suspensions and grant you permission to return to Class 1-A!"

She stamped three documents she had on her desk.

"Thank you, Chairwoman," I said.

"Hooray!" exclaimed Lia.

"We can finally get back to our real studies," added Rose.

Though I was worried about being a full month behind, more than that, I was just happy and excited to be back.

I'm finally here. I can take the Soul Attire class at last!

I'd seen many different examples of Soul Attire in a short period of time—Lia's Dragon King Fafnir, Cain's Hundred Hellblade, Shido's Ice Wolf Vanargand, Dodriel's Shadow Sovereign, and Rize's Withered Umbrella—and each one of them had tremendously powerful abilities.

I wonder what kind of ability mine will have...

That was all I could think about last night, so I didn't end up getting much sleep.

"Anyway, first period is about to begin. Hmm... It starts in ten minutes, so I'll just walk with you three," said Reia.

We walked to Class 1-A together with her. It felt a little nostalgic heading down the hallways for the first time in a month.

"And we're here," the chairwoman announced.

She took one step to the side instead of opening the door. It looked like she wanted us to go in first.

"Phew..."

I exhaled loudly.

"I-I'm a little nervous...," admitted Lia.

"Yeah, it's been a month since we've seen everyone...," agreed Rose.

That was part of the reason I was anxious about seeing my classmates, but most of all, I didn't know how I was going to face them.

I've caused so much trouble for everyone...

I regretted what had happened during my match with Shido in the Elite Five Holy Festival.

If only I'd been able to control that power without my Spirit Core taking me over...

We probably would have defeated Ice King Academy, our longtime rival, if that hadn't been the case. Honestly, I found myself ruminating on those kinds of what-ifs all the time.

"Okay...I'm going in. Ready?" I asked for confirmation. Lia and Rose nodded.

Steeling myself for the cold glares and jeers of my classmates, I slowly opened the door.

""""CONGRATULATIONS ON YOUR RETURN, ALLEN, LIA, AND ROSE!"""""

Our classmates fired off party crackers and shouted their congratulations.

"""""...Huh?""""" all three of us mumbled in surprise, staring open-mouthed at this unexpected development.

"Ah-ha-ha-ha! You should see your faces!"

"That couldn't have gone better!"

"Welcome back! The last month must have been hard!"

Our classmates rushed toward us.

"U-um...you're not mad?" I asked, voicing my fear.

"Of course not! Your opponent went way too far! Plus, he was an asshole!"

"It felt great seeing you beat the hell out of him!"

"You *did* go a bit overboard in the end, though!"

Everyone gave us a warm welcome.

Man...

I could feel tears welling up. Crying in front of this many people would have been embarrassing, though, so I did my best to stave them off. Meanwhile, our classmates threw questions at us in rapid succession.

"You worked as witchblades while you were suspended, right? Tell us about it!"

"I heard a rumor that there's a terrifying bald dude at the Aurest Witchblade Guild... Was it scary working there?"

"Oh yeah, I wanna hear about the incident at the Unity Festival! Rize Dorhein name-dropped you in an interview, Allen!"

"U-um..."

I was flustered by the barrage of questions.

"Hold on, kids. Save the stories for later. We've already cut into class time," Chairwoman Reia said, pointing at the wall clock above the blackboard.

I looked at the clock and saw that it was already three minutes past the start of the period.

"Ah, shoot, guess we have to."

"We'll talk later, okay?"

Our classmates returned to their seats while muttering complaints under their breath. Lia, Rose, and I sat at our regular desks by the windows. The chairwoman stood behind her podium and announced something that didn't make any sense.

"All right, today marks the start of our Soul Attire class!"

What?

"Whooo! I've been so excited!"

"The last month was really hard…"

"It's finally time to see what my Soul Attire is capable of!"

My classmates all cheered as if they'd been waiting for this day.

"Ch-Chairwoman? What do you mean by that?" I asked.

"Hmm? Oh, I haven't told you yet… Per the wishes of your classmates, we've been doing nothing but strength training for the last month until your suspensions ended. They insisted on starting Soul Attire lessons at the same time as you three," Reia explained.

"H-huh?!"

I looked toward my peers, and they all smiled and nodded.

I'm overjoyed *that I'll be able to learn Soul Attire together with everyone…*

Studying with just Lia and Rose would have been fine, too, but not nearly as exciting as practicing with the whole class.

I feel bad about making them waste an entire month of their lives, though.

The guilt I felt greatly surpassed my happiness. Then as if she could read my mind, the chairwoman smiled boldly.

"Don't get the wrong idea, Allen. Your classmates didn't squander a single second of their time," she mentioned.

"Wh-what do you mean?" I asked.

"I personally pushed them like you wouldn't believe for the entire month! See for yourself. Haven't they all bulked up since the last time you saw them?"

"...Hmm."

Now that I thought about it, everyone was in significantly better shape than they were a month ago.

They're not at the level of Ms. Paula or Mr. Bonz, but it's still impressive.

The guys had added a lot of muscle, and I could see that the girls' legs had become more toned.

Strength was the basis for all swordcraft. To give an extreme example, if a five-year-old prodigy were to clash with a ripped novice, the novice would undoubtedly come out on top. That was how important improving your body was.

"Heh-heh, I'll have no trouble keeping up with you now, Allen!"

"I've overcome a month of hellish training and improved my Slice Iron Style even further. I'm a brand-new man!"

"You have to give us a match later!"

It was the three boys whom I'd dueled on the first day of class. They each laughed confidently.

"Sure, anytime!" I responded.

It seemed like I was just overthinking things. Everyone in this room had significantly more talent with the blade than I did. There was no way they would choose to waste an entire month of their lives.

"Let's get started! We're moving to the Soul Attire Room—follow me!" announced Chairwoman Reia.

And so we followed her outside the classroom.

■

We arrived at the Soul Attire Room, which was an underground facility.

"All right, everyone, go to the prep room and grab a soul-crystal sword!" Chairwoman Reia ordered before blowing the shrill whistle hanging from her neck. This was giving me déjà vu.

"Let's go, Allen!"

"The prep room is…over there."

Lia and Rose took my hands and led me inside.

"Let's see… They're over there!"

"Wow, they're beautiful."

They both quickly grabbed one of the many soul-crystal swords stored in the room.

These blades were made with a rare mineral called soul crystals. They were used in Soul Attire classes and could apparently induce a person's Spirit Core to rise to the surface.

I followed their example and took one of the weapons.

It's heavier than I expected.

The blade looked like it was constructed out of transparent blue glass, but it was a good amount heavier than a regular sword. After collecting our gear, we left the prep room so we wouldn't get in anyone's way, then returned to the center of the Soul Attire Room, where the chairwoman was waiting.

The next moment, a brilliant idea popped into my head.

Doing some practice swings with this sword would make for great training!

Its weight would surely double or triple the results of my practice swings, which would do wonders for my shoulder muscles, core, and back muscles. I performed a few light slashes as a warm-up.

"Word of warning, these soul-crystal swords are very expensive. Each one is worth one million guld, so I suggest you handle them with care," the chairwoman shouted conspicuously enough for everyone to hear.

"O-one million guld?!"

Floored by the exorbitant price tag, I immediately stopped what I was doing.

How can a single blade be worth that much?!

Clutching my weapon cautiously in both of my hands, I quickly glanced around. I counted thirty soul-crystal swords total, which meant there was thirty million guld worth of gear in this room alone. That was enough money to live worry-free for a decade.

This place isn't one of the Elite Five Academies for nothing...

The equipment and facilities here were truly stunning.

As my face went pale, the rest of my classmates waved their swords around without a care in the world.

They all must be loaded...

That should have been a given. Every one of them was an elite sword wielder who'd graduated from a famous swordcraft academy. None of them were born in the sticks like I was.

The thought made me feel more than a little out of place.

"Nrgh..."

"Ahhh..."

Lia and Rose, who were both holding their soul-crystal swords, suddenly each made a sensual-sounding noise. Their cheeks were slightly flushed, and they were fidgeting restlessly.

"Uh, are you two okay?" I asked.

"S-sorry, Allen. I don't know why I made that voice...," answered Lia.

"My body is so hot... I feel odd...," muttered Rose.

Swaying a little, they looked down at their blades.

...They feel odd?

I wasn't sure what Rose meant, but they were clearly acting strangely.

Their faces are red... Do they have a fever?

I contemplated whether I should take them to the infirmary or alert Chairwoman Reia about it. Before I could decide what to do, however, the chairwoman blew her whistle.

"Okay, is everyone ready?"

She swept her eyes across the class, then gave a satisfied nod.

"I'm sure some of you know this already, but soul-crystal swords are special weapons that are only used for acquiring Soul Attire. Just holding one gives you a strange sensation, doesn't it?"

My classmates all bobbed their heads together. Everyone had the same symptoms as Lia and Rose to some extent.

Hmm... I really don't feel much of anything.

It seemed like I was the only one in the class who was totally unaffected.

"When a talented sword wielder like each of you holds one of these blades, you should begin to feel a throbbing inside your body. This is proof that the Spirit Core dwelling within you has been stimulated. The intensity of the throbbing differs greatly depending on the person, but generally speaking, the response is stronger in women than in men."

It sounded like talent vastly influenced your level of pulsations.

That's something I've always lacked...

There could be no better explanation for why I felt nothing.

"What I want you all to do now is begin a dialogue with the Spirit Core concealed within your soul. You should speak with it, duel it, negotiate with it, and ultimately seize its power. The ability you gain will be a manifestation of a piece of your Spirit Core, which becomes your Soul Attire!"

I was at last connecting the dots on a subject I'd only ever had a vague grasp of; I was very grateful that Reia had explained it in a way that was so easy to understand.

"There's one thing I need to warn you of—make sure you don't let it take control," the chairwoman said, lowering her voice. "The fundamental purpose of a Spirit Core is to protect you. You are mostly safe to think of it as your ally. However, there are very rare instances where your Spirit Core has such a strong sense of self that it will try to possess your body. As you all are aware, Allen's is one such example."

Every one of my peers turned to me.

"That being said, his is especially abnormal—a rarity among rarities. Your Spirit Core will almost never try to possess you, so there's not much need to worry about that. On the off chance that it does take over, however, I'll subdue it," she insisted, cracking the knuckles of her right hand.

That's reassuring.

The chairwoman was definitely unreliable about paperwork, but when it came to matters of muscle, her presence was more than appreciated.

"Anyway, let's move on to the explanation. Using soul-crystal swords couldn't be simpler! Start by closing your eyes and focusing your mind. Then sink deeper and deeper into your consciousness until you reach the world of your soul. Before you know it, your Spirit Core will be right in front of you."

It was an abstract, yet intuitive explanation.

"Well, I think seeing is believing with this one. Go ahead and try it."

Chairwoman Reia then clapped her hands together and told us to begin. Everyone in the class closed their eyes and started to concentrate.

Okay, let's do this.

Honestly, I was a little frightened. The possibility that *he* might hijack my body and wreak havoc again was making me nervous.

Chairwoman Reia said she would use her might to suppress us, though.

If worse came to worst, I was sure she would bring me down.

"Whew"

After exhaling deeply, I sank into the depths of my consciousness until I reached the world of my soul. The minutes passed slowly. But before I knew it, he was right there in front of me.

"Yo, it's been a while."

He had long white hair, and a black mark on his face. His expression was so savage that I felt like he could eat somebody. Most unsettling of all, he had my face.

This was my Spirit Core.

◼

I was in a sprawling, desolate world with rotten vegetation, putrid soil, and fetid air. *He* was sitting there alone on a giant, cracked rock.

"You really are my Spirit Core...," I remarked.

"Huh? Oh...sure, you can think of me that way," he answered evasively. "So whaddaya want? Finally feel like handing over that body?"

He aggressively changed the subject.

"Of course not. You would just go on another rampage if I did that," I answered.

"Gya-ha-ha-ha! That's better than having power and choosing not to wield it, like you. I'll never understand it. Letting loose, crushing people, and kicking back is what life is all about! You need to live for the moment!"

Personally, I wasn't a huge fan of that moment-to-moment behavior.

"That's not the lifestyle for me. I'd rather live a long, simple existence," I stated.

"Geez, you're so goddamn boring..." He sighed, shrugging.

"Anyway, I'm never going to give up my body. After what you did last time, why would I?"

He'd pushed Shido to the brink of death. If Lia hadn't stopped me, my Spirit Core would have slaughtered him without hesitation.

"You mean when I fought that ice-wielding brat? Sure, I went a little overboard, but think about it. That saved your life."

"I...can't deny that."

He definitely had rescued me during my bout with Shido. I didn't have any energy left to dodge when Shido had lunged for my throat with the move he called Vanar Thrust. If my Spirit Core hadn't emerged, there's no question I would be in the ground right about now.

"You have no idea how grueling that was... I had to possess your body with the path still closed. I'm still stupid tired from the enormous amount of power I had to use."

He gave a big yawn. I didn't have a clue what he was going on about.

"Regardless, you should be grateful. You have no business blaming me for what I did," he chided.

"Okay...thank you," I responded.

Though I wanted to tell him that he'd gone too far and that he shouldn't have gotten so violent, I did have to express my gratitude to him for saving my life.

"Huh? Gross, don't get all sappy with me. Thank me with your actions instead—gimme that vessel of yours," he asked again. Something about this constant request didn't make sense to me.

"You really seem to want my consent. You're clearly strong enough to take my body by force, though," I countered.

"How stupid are you? With the path closed, overtaking your flesh with your consent—without any resistance—consumes significantly less energy than twisting your will and controlling it by force! I'm just a spirit, after all...," he explained before looking at his right hand with a frown.

"Oh, I see..."

That was a relief to hear. Just as Chairwoman Reia had told us, he'd made a great sacrifice when he'd possessed me.

That means he can't just take over me whenever he wants...! I thought.

"If you're not gonna give me your body, then get lost. I'm sick of your ugly mug."

He waved his hand as if swatting away a fly. What a selfish guy.

"I'm not leaving. I came to borrow your power. You know why I'm here—I want to obtain my Soul Attire," I insisted.

I decided I should try starting a dialogue first. He was crazy, but clearly not an idiot. He could speak intelligently, and most importantly, he was capable of rational thought. If I spoke with him or negotiated with him, there was a chance I could get him to lend me a part of his might.

"Huh? You're saying I should give an amateur like you a piece of my power? *Pfft*, gya-ha-ha-ha-ha! That's a good one!"

My Spirit Core slapped his knees and burst out laughing.

"H-hey! That wasn't a joke—"

"Cut the bullshit!"

Before I knew it, he was standing right in front of my face.

"...?!"

He'd already lifted his right arm and was going to nail me in less than a second.

"Take this!"

He delivered a right straight, with no feint.

"?!"

On a split-second impulse, I slipped my sword between my face and his arm. It was a perfect defense. I dropped my center of gravity and prepared for impact.

To my surprise, however, he sent me rocketing backward as if I were a ball.

What the...? He's ridiculously strong!

My defensive move hadn't worked at all. I twirled in midair to bring myself to a halt, then brandished my blade as soon as I landed.

"Geez, how little do you weigh...? Are you skipping meals, dumbass?!"

"...I'm eating just fine."

His blows were impossible to defend against.

That means all I need to do is stay on the offensive and not give him a chance to strike!

I closed the large gap between us with one step and unleashed my signature chain of slashes.

"Eighth Style—Eight-Span Crow!"

My eight-strike attack had become much stronger since my encounter with Shido. Despite that, my Spirit Core just yawned. A moment later, my eight slashes rained down on his arms, legs, neck, head, torso, and the rest of his body.

Unlike when I'd fought Dodriel, I felt each move connect. And yet, not a single one did so much as scratch him.

How is that possible?!

Not only could I not cut through his skin, but I also hadn't even left a single bruise. In fact, my blade seemed like it was going to break instead.

"Pathetic...do you really think you can hurt me with such a childish skill?" he taunted, totally at ease.

Crap, I don't stand a chance...

His upper-body strength, lower-body strength, and stamina were like nothing I'd ever seen.

I continued to slash at him, but he batted all my attacks away with his right hand without a care in the world.

It's no use... It doesn't matter if I hit his face, neck, solar plexus, or any other vital point; I can't bring him down with normal strikes.

But that didn't mean I was out of options. I still had a certain move up my sleeve.

There's no way my special ability that can tear through a world won't hurt him.

Waiting for an opening, I delivered a series of moderate slices. When he yawned as if tired of our duel, I struck.

"Fifth Style—World Render!"

My strongest attack, so powerful that it tore through the World of Time, ended in failure.

"Good lord, could you be any slower? You're gonna put me to sleep."

"You can't be serious..."

Unbelievably, he grabbed my blade before I could even swing it down. This guy was a monster.

"Down here, the strength of your heart determines your power. A total amateur like you couldn't hope to have the resolve to fight me!"

I was totally defenseless as he held my sword, then he kicked me hard in the stomach.

"Gah!"

My breath shot from my lungs, and blood rushed to my head. My vision flickered, and I lost my sense of balance completely. He cackled as he watched me tumble to the ground.

"Ha-ha-ha! Now that your will has been weakened, I'll take that vessel of yours!"

"No...don't..."

My consciousness faded to black.

■

The moment Allen lost to his Spirit Core, his body began to transform. His black hair grew long and turned white, and a black pattern appeared under his left eye. What was most striking, however, was his change in demeanor. His kind and gentle manner disappeared, replaced by the menacing sharpness of a bare blade.

"Gya-ha-ha-ha-ha! That was way too easy, you bra— Whuh?!"

While he celebrated his victory over Allen, Reia appeared before him with clenched black fists.

"Swordless Style—Sever!"

"Gwah!"

Reia hit him hard in the abdomen with a powerful thrust that exceeded the speed of sound.

"Spirit Cores have one major weakness—they can't move freely until they wrest total control from their host. This period is called 'initial petrification,'" Reia explained.

Allen staggered a few steps backward, then looked at her with eyes full of hate.

"B-Black Fist…it's you…," he spat.

"I'm impressed you can manage this endurance in such an *immature body*… You really are a monster," observed Reia.

"Shit…"

Allen lost consciousness, and the changes to his body immediately vanished.

"I don't like resorting to such a dirty trick, but think of that as a handicap. Truly subduing you would be tough even for me…"

The Soul Attire Room fell dead quiet. Lia then asked the question on everyone's mind.

"Reia, was that…?"

"Yeah, that was Allen's Spirit Core. As you witnessed, it's terrifyingly powerful. Allen Rodol has a preposterous amount of talent. It's honestly a little frightening, but as his teacher, I am excited to watch his growth," she responded, shaking her bloodied right hand.

"Is that blood…?"

"Hmm? Oh, you can relax. It's mine. My hand didn't even get *this* battered when I leveled three mountains. Allen's stomach is relatively soft. I'm stunned by how firm it had gotten."

After learning that Reia's right hand wasn't seriously injured, Lia finally asked what had been gnawing at her the most.

"Is Allen okay?"

"Of course. He'll wake up soon, so there's no need to worry. Anyway, let's get back to it! Concentrate so you can acquire your Soul Attire!"

She then blew the whistle that she was so fond of.

■

I was lying flat on my back when I came to after losing to my Spirit Core.

"Urgh… Where am I?"

Lifting up my upper body, I saw Chairwoman Reia standing right next to me.

"Hey, you've already come to. I knew you would recover quickly," she said.

"Ch-Chairwoman…? Oh yeah! What happened with that—that monster?!" I asked.

I was positive I'd heard him say, *"I'll take that vessel of yours,"* as my consciousness faded. Flustered, I looked around the room but didn't see any signs of violence.

"Don't worry. I knocked him out right away. I had to be a bit underhanded, though," she answered with a look of frustration. It sounded like she'd stooped to a method she would have preferred not to have used.

Regardless of how she'd pulled it off, however, I was just grateful that she'd stopped him from doing any damage.

"Sorry about that," I said.

"No need to apologize. I expected this to happen," she responded with a smile, clapping me on the back.

Now that things had settled down, I took a moment to reflect.

The strength of my mind…

He'd told me that your power in that place depended on "the strength of your heart," and that I didn't have the "resolve" to fight him. In order to defeat him in that world, and in order to obtain my Soul Attire, I would apparently need to train my heart.

But how do you do that?

Figuring out how to hone your body and your sword skills isn't rocket science. You can perform practice swings or have someone teach you some techniques. Edifying your heart, however, is very difficult.

Should I meditate? Stand under a waterfall? I'm not sure what to do...

I racked my brain until the chairwoman interrupted me.

"Allen, this is your chance!" she suddenly exclaimed, clapping her hands.

"Wh-what do you mean?"

"It takes an enormous amount of energy for a Spirit Core to manifest against their host's wishes. Now might be your best shot to tear away his power!"

"Should I fight him again?"

"Of course. Come on, ready your soul-crystal sword! Don't let this opportunity go to waste!"

She took my hands and tightened them on the grip of my blade.

"B-but...what if he gets loose again?"

"I'll just subdue him. But I don't think he'll emerge again today. Given the nature of Spirit Cores, I'm positive that he's vulnerable right now. There'll be no problem as long as I keep a watchful eye on you."

She paused and then gave me one warning.

"But make sure you don't go near him while I'm not around, okay?"

"..."

Her tone was firm and serious.

"Allen, your Spirit Core is monstrous—literally in another category entirely. You just clashed with him, so you should know that better than anyone."

"...Yeah."

His power really was on a whole different level.

"If he's not trounced during his period of initial petrification—a weakness that all Spirit Cores share—even I don't know what would happen. That's why I only want you to practice your Soul Attire where I can keep an eye on you. As long as I'm around, it won't matter if he manages to take over. I'll stop him every time," she assured me.

"...Yes, ma'am. Please watch over me."

"Sure thing."

After that, I challenged my Spirit Core repeatedly, but his might proved too much for me. Ultimately, every attempt failed miserably. On the bright side, he didn't possess me again after that first instance. I was also happy to see that he'd weakened even slightly. True to Reia's word, it seemed that he required an enormous amount of energy to control my body.

No matter how many times I confront him, though, I still have no chance of defeating him.

I needed to develop my heart.

"Chairwoman Reia, how does one strengthen—?"

My question was interrupted.

"Hey, we've come here to demand a duel!"

The door to the Soul Attire Room flung open, and a group of five people entered. They were all wearing Thousand Blade Academy uniforms, and I'd seen some of them in this building. They were likely fellow first-years.

"All right, where's the third-rate swordsman named Allen Rodol?"

Sounded like they were here for me.

■

Two teachers burst into the Soul Attire Room immediately after the group of five students waltzed in.

"I-I'm so sorry, Chairwoman!"

"What are you kids thinking? We're in the middle of class right now!"

Surprisingly, the chairwoman stopped the instructors.

"I don't mind. I like to see fire in my wards... When I was a first-year, I was left off the team for the Holy Festival. As soon as I heard, I challenged one of the participants to a duel and claimed their spot for myself," she told them.

"R-really...?"

It sounded like she'd been a handful when she was a student, too.

"Thousand Blade Academy had such a grand atmosphere back then. You'd find sparring matches and duels playing out everywhere you looked! Oh, those were the days!" she reminisced.

Bickering and getting into fights with other students nonstop doesn't sound appealing to me.

Personally, I'd rather get along with everyone and have fun as we honed our swordcraft together. As I thought that over, the boy at the front of the invading band drew his blade.

"Where are you, Allen Rodol? Too scared to announce yourself?" he spat provokingly, sweeping his eyes across the class.

"That's Reyes... He wields a scimitar," whispered one of my classmates.

"You mean Reyes Volgan, the one who caused so much trouble in middle school? I had no idea he enrolled here," whispered another.

Reyes Volgan... Sounds like he has a bad reputation.

His hair was dark red, and a bit long for a boy. A silver earring hung from his left ear, and he stood slightly taller than me at about 170 centimeters.

We weren't going to get anywhere if I stayed quiet, so I decided to speak up.

"I'm Allen Rodol. What do you want from me?"

"Hmm..."

The five of them examined me appraisingly.

"Ha-ha-ha! You're tellin' me this deadbeat was chosen to compete in the prestigious Elite Five Holy Festival?"

"Did he bribe someone?"

"There's no way a wuss like him could be a good swordsman."

"He looks so frail."

"Well, clearly, he's no threat to us."

They bombarded me with insults; obviously, they weren't impressed with me.

"You all had better watch it!" Lia fired back.

"You're obviously blind," warned Rose.

The girls both glared at the five students. Reyes paid them no mind, however, and produced a piece of paper from his pocket.

"I did some research into you, Allen Rodol. You were a total failure at Grand Swordcraft Academy. Students even called you the Reject Swordsman, and you had the worst grades in the history of your institution. You tried to join many Schools of Swordcraft, but their teachers all turned you away because of your impressive lack of talent. That's why you're self-taught! I also read that in your third year, you defeated some swordsman named Dodriel by using a cheap trick."

There was no doubt that he did some thorough research into my time at Grand Swordcraft Academy. But so what? The past was just that—the past. There was no point comparing my current self with who I was from a billion years ago.

"Do you all realize now what an unskilled poser Allen is? Wake up, you idiots! The Reject Swordsman is deceiving you! Or does he have something on everyone here? Is it money?" Reyes accused.

My classmates in Class 1-A couldn't hold back their laughter any longer.

"Sheesh, guys… Did you not see Allen's fight against Shido?" a classmate asked, shrugging in disbelief.

"I saw it. He got thrashed in the beginning, then right after, he finally started to show some fight, and his Spirit Core possessed him, so he got eliminated for breaking the rules! Is that supposed to impress me?"

Reyes guffawed scornfully, and then the other four spoke up in turn.

"You may be Class 1-A, but that's only based on your skill from when we entered the academy."

"Yeah, that's no reason to act like you're better than us."

"I don't know about this cheap friendship thing you guys have going on, but you're all idiots for spending the last month doing boring strength training instead of taking your Soul Attire class. You're no match for us."

"The strength of a swordfighter is the strength of their Soul Attire. Everyone knows that."

Every one of them was mocking us.

I can't let them get away with this.

I couldn't just stand by without brandishing my blade as I watched them ridicule my friends. I took a step forward.

"Wait, Allen."

Tessa Balmond, the boy who practiced the Slice Iron School of Swordcraft, leaped out in front of me.

"There's no need for you to face these jerks. Leave them to me. I'll cut them down with my Slice Iron Style!"

He drew his weapon emphatically.

"Hmm, what's this? You goin' first?" Reyes asked provokingly.

"Yeah, I'll give you your fight. But we're not going to need a second against the likes of you," Tessa boasted confidently.

"…Heh, how funny. Fine, let's do this. Come at me!"

Looking offended, Reyes calmly drew his scimitar.

"" …""

As they locked eyes, the atmosphere turned menacing.

Ten seconds passed, then another ten…

"Slice Iron Style—Rust Remover!"

Tessa dashed straight forward and swung his blade at Reyes.

That's a good strike!

He'd devoted himself to physical conditioning last month, and the fruits of his training were plain to see. His grip, charge, and vigor had all improved significantly.

"Hyaaaaaaaa!" he screamed as he swung his sword.

Reyes grinned in the face of Tessa's slash attack.

"Surge Forth—Three Skeledragons!"

Suddenly, three small dragons materialized and blocked Tessa's strike.

"What?!"

Each one of the skeletal wyrms, whose eye sockets shone with red light, chortled merrily.

"See if you can handle this. Skeleton Shower!"

His three familiars broke apart into small bones and flew at Tessa with stunning speed.

"Gah!!!"

The projectiles pelted Tessa and knocked him backward onto the ground, where he fell unconscious.

"T-Tessa!"

"Are you okay?!"

"Someone take him to the infirmary!"

Reyes watched as my classmates began to panic.

"*Pfft*, ah-ha-ha-ha-ha! How pathetic! Is everyone in Class 1-A this feeble?" he shouted, clapping his hands and bellowing with laughter. The four students behind him jeered at Tessa as well.

...*Damn.*

In terms of pure swordcraft, Tessa was much more skilled.

But Reyes is currently the superior swordsman.

And only one thing set him apart—Soul Attire.

Whether or not a sword wielder could produce Soul Attire made an enormous difference. In fact, you had to actually be able to control this ability in order to become a high-ranking holy knight. That was how much society valued the power of Soul Attire.

As we were preoccupied worrying about Tessa, the other four students sprang to action.

"Indent—Adamantine Blade!"

"Envelope—Shorea Robusta!"

"Come Out and Play—Flame Children!"

"Pierce—Eyeleteer!"

They each produced their Soul Attire.

"Are you serious?!"

"This whole group obtained their Soul Attire in just one month?!"

"Crap, guess they weren't all talk..."

My classmates were starting to freak out. In response, I calmly drew my sword and approached the interlopers.

"I'll help, Allen!"

"I want to fight, too!"

Lia and Rose both rushed forward to back me up.

"Actually, can you let me do this alone?"

"A-are you insane?! All five of them have Soul Attire!"

"No matter how strong you are, you can't possibly beat every one of them by yourself!"

They were definitely right, but they weren't going to change my mind.

"Sorry. I just really want to do this on my own."

"...Okay, fine. But don't do anything rash!"

"Withdraw the moment it's clear you can't win."

Seeing that my mind was set on this, Lia and Rose reluctantly stepped back.

"Thanks."

I exhaled, then glared at the five students in front of me.

They can say whatever they want about me. It's true that I'm the Reject Swordsman, and true that I have no talent. There's no point denying any of that at this juncture.

But my classmates were different. They were all elite sword wielders with innate talent who'd put painstaking effort into their skills. And more than anything, they'd been nice enough to delay the beginning of our Soul Attire course for the likes of me.

I can't just sit back and watch as they ridicule my friends.

My peers weren't weak by any stretch of the imagination. There was no way that these hardworking prodigies, who'd spent an entire month performing dull, demanding physical conditioning, could be considered frail.

I need to get Reyes and the others to see that they're wrong...

And there was one method that would be most effective for making them understand.

If all five of them lose to the Reject Swordsman, they'll be completely out of arguments.

To force them to admit that they were mistaken, I, the Reject Swordsman, would have to take the whole group on and strike them down myself.

This is for Class 1-A! I can't lose!

As I fortified myself, I felt something strange—the inside of my body seemed to grow hot, and I sensed power surge within me.

Oh, I see... This must be what resolve *feels like.*

It was as though I'd gotten a glimmer of insight into what my Spirit Core had told me. This feeling that I couldn't afford to fail, the determination to fight for everyone's sake, and the eagerness to represent my class all combined to strengthen my heart and open the path to my Soul Attire.

As I basked in the energy flowing through me, the five challengers began to berate me.

"Heh, finally decided to show yourself, Reject Swordsman?"

"Hmm-hmm, we'll let you off if you cry and apologize."

"Whoa, are you really gonna try and fight us alone?"

"Talk about idiocy. This just feels like bullying..."

"You truly have no idea how far we outstrip you... How comical."

They each readied their Soul Attire and smiled fearlessly. I could see in their eyes that they couldn't be surer of their imminent victory.

...Something feels off.

I felt no aura whatsoever from their Soul Attire. When I'd duked it out with my Spirit Core, it was as if my heart were being squeezed, but now I sensed absolutely nothing. Their Soul Attires were utterly lifeless.

I assumed the middle stance and raised my voice.

"Ready?"

"Ha-ha, go ahead. We'll cut through you like cloth!"

Reyes shrugged and laughed.

"...Huh?"

I closed the distance between us instantly and pulverized his three dragons with a single strike. The bones clattered to his feet, and a momentary silence befell the five students.

"What the hell was that?!" Reyes exclaimed, flabbergasted.

"You're finished," I asserted, and I struck his open neck with the back of my sword.

"Impossible…"

His eyes rolled into the back of his head, and he collapsed.

""""…?!"""""

The other four students went pale.

"Bone Crusher!"

"Shorea Snare!"

"Fire Daruma!"

"Puncture!"

They each psyched themselves up by unleashing the power of their Soul Attire, and then they proceeded to attack me at once.

But I was ready for them.

"Eighth Style—Eight-Span Crow!"

I knocked each of their Soul Attire weapons away with my eight slash attacks.

"Huh?!"

"No way…"

"He defeated us…alone?"

"I don't understand…"

They muttered to themselves deliriously as they watched their Soul Attire vanish before their eyes.

"Soul Attire is certainly very powerful. But if the person wielding it lacks skill, they won't be able to make full use of it," I said.

Take Shido's Vanargand, for instance. Shido could cause so much destruction when he wielded it because of his overwhelming physical strength. If Reyes were to use it, he wouldn't have posed nearly as much of a threat.

I sheathed my blade, and they all collapsed on the spot. They probably hadn't even noticed that I'd hit each of them on the neck directly after Eight-Span Crow.

"In other words, your training is simply insufficient," I finished.

I'd successfully repelled my sudden challengers.

CHAPTER 3

Recruiting & the Group of Weirdos

One week had passed since the duel with Reyes Volgan.

Every day followed the same routine—we spent all our time in class on Soul Attire training, I devoted myself to swinging my sword after school, and once I got home, I performed strict physical conditioning. My days were exhausting but fulfilling.

I'm still a long way from obtaining my Soul Attire...

Every time I faced my Spirit Core, I ended up losing miserably.

...but that doesn't mean I've made no progress.

Although my Spirit Core was so strong that he seemed invincible, in the last few days, he'd begun to occasionally dodge my blade. He did so about once out of every hundred attacks. Now I could pull off slashes that left even me impressed, and those were always the ones he dodged.

He probably evades them because he thinks I'll actually hurt him.

The mere thought raised my spirits. I couldn't even dent him before, but now I was actually capable of causing him pain. I felt like I'd truly grown. This was the same happiness from when I'd first cut through the space of the World of Time.

If I keep practicing, I'll definitely be able to defeat him someday. And then I'll finally be able to manifest my Soul Attire!

My chest swelled with hope as I waited for Lia by the dorm entrance. She arrived a few minutes later.

"Sorry, Allen. I overslept a bit."

She rushed toward me with an apologetic expression.

"It's fine, we have time."

First period started in fifteen minutes. Our dorm was located on campus, so our classroom was only five minutes away. We still had plenty of leeway.

"Are you feeling okay? You haven't been sleeping well lately," I asked.

Her rest had been a little rough since around the time we'd started taking the Soul Attire course. She always whimpered and thrashed in bed after nodding off.

"U-um...can you please not watch me while I sleep...?" Lia responded, blushing and staring at the ground.

"Oh, uh, s-sorry about that..."

That was probably a rude thing to say to a girl your age. I struggled for some words to follow up with, but Lia spoke up before I could.

"D-did I make any weird faces...?" she asked timidly.

"No, don't worry about that. You always look beautiful when you're sleeping," I assured her.

"Oh, uh...th-thank you..."

"..."

"..."

Lia fell quiet, and I followed suit. A strange atmosphere befell us that made it difficult to talk. The ticking from the second hand of the clock on the wall felt absurdly loud.

This is awkward... I'm the one responsible for this, so I need to find a way to fix it! I thought.

What should I do?! This just got really uncomfortable! thought Lia.

I finally broke the silence by speaking in an overly loud and forced voice.

"I-it's almost time to go! Let's get to class!"

"S-sure, let's go!"

Lia jumped on my suggestion, and we escaped from our odd deadlock. With a weird tension still hanging between us, we headed for Class 1-A.

A surprise greeted us when we arrived on campus.

"Swimming Club! Come join the Swimming Club!"

"Wanna master the blade? The Swordcraft Club would be perfect for you!"

"Run to your heart's content with the Track-and-Field Club! Come and feel the wind on your face!"

Some upperclassmen who were wearing a variety of outfits, including competition swimsuits, martial-arts robes, and athletic shorts, handed us countless flyers.

"Wh-what's going on?" I asked.

"I think they're recruiting for clubs?" Lia answered.

We were both befuddled by the unusual sight.

"Wow, you're really fit! You should join the Judo Club!"

"Omigod, you're so cute! Wanna join the Cheerleading Club?! We have lots of adorable outfits!"

"Hey, you two, how about the Mountaineering Club? Nothing beats the scenery of a steep mountain you just hiked!"

Even more upperclassmen swarmed us and shoved flyers into our hands.

"H-huh?! Me...?!"

"L-let's go, Lia!"

I took her hand, and we ran for the main building. It looked like recruiting was forbidden indoors, so they moved on to the next target.

"Phew..."

"Th-that startled me..."

Only now did I notice that they'd stuffed my unform pockets chock-full of handouts. They'd shoved a ridiculous number of leaflets into Lia's free left hand as well.

"They're recruiting, aren't they?" I mused.

"I think so...," Lia responded.

We moved on to the classroom and entered to find our classmates looking like they'd finished a marathon.

"I guess they all went through the same thing."

"Seems that way…"

They must have met some fierce recruiting to end up this exhausted.

Lia and I sat in our usual places, and Tessa approached me, looking dejected.

"Hey, Allen. Did they get you, too?" he asked.

"Yeah. I can see you also got it rough…"

He looked pale. The dense stack of flyers on his desk told a tale of great mental damage.

"Heh-heh, isn't that insane? Almost all those are for the Judo Club. Apparently, I have a perfect body for the sport," Tessa said, pointing at his desk with a pained smile. "I thought I was gonna die back there. I was just walking to class when ten sweaty upperclassmen all wearing judo uniforms jumped me out of nowhere. They stank so much that I almost passed out…"

"Th-that sounds awful."

Just imagining that felt like hell.

The New Student–Recruiting Period—or just *Recruiting* for short— began in May at Thousand Blade Academy and the other Elite Five Academies. Chairwoman Reia had told us about it beforehand. She'd said that recruiting for new clubs was prohibited for the first month of the school year in April so that new students could focus on Soul Attire lessons.

"We have to put up with this for another week. They're gonna pounce on us when we go to and from school, and at lunch, too. We're not gonna get a break. Good luck to us all, I guess…," Tessa said gloomily, sitting down at his desk, which had been converted into a tower of Judo Club flyers.

"This is going to be a nightmare…," I muttered.

"I'd heard that Recruiting at the Elite Five Academies was crazy, but I never would have imagined this," shared Lia.

The door rattled open, and a mass of leaflets walked into the room. I couldn't tell who was inside it, but they had obviously suffered greatly.

The pile of handouts slowly approached us and sat in the seat in front of me.

"...Phoo."

Rose's face emerged from the mountain of flyers. As per usual, she had an impressive case of bedhead. She was a horrible morning person, so she'd probably staggered to class half asleep and ended up like this before she knew what had hit her.

"Good morning, Rose. They really took it out on you," I remarked.

"I think you got more leaflets than anyone in the whole class," observed Lia.

We struggled to hold back our laughter.

"Nnrgh, *yawn*... Mornin'," Rose responded.

She stretched and yawned. Her extreme drowsiness apparently outweighed her annoyance at the papers.

"Recruiting is so intense... Which clubs are you joining?" Rose asked, rubbing her eyes and changing the subject.

"Honestly, I still haven't decided on one," I responded.

"I haven't found any tempting options yet, either," added Lia.

I did want to enter a club to experience one of the joys of student life, but currently, I didn't see any that spoke to me. The only one I had any interest in was the Swordcraft Club, but that was simply because of the name.

"Oh, good. I actually haven't settled on anything as well. Want to go look around together after school?" offered Rose.

"Sounds great," I answered.

"Yeah, let's do it!" added Lia.

Just like that, we'd made plans to walk around and survey the clubs after school.

■

We performed strict Soul Attire training under Chairwoman Reia's supervision from first to fifth period, then wrapped up the day with afternoon homeroom. Lia, Rose, and I were currently taking a rest in our classroom.

"Man, that was another long day," I grumbled after exhaling deeply.

"Soul Attire class is more draining mentally than it is physically," said Lia.

"I feel dead," expressed Rose.

They both took a sip from their water bottles.

We spent some time resting in our seats. Once we'd recovered enough from our exhaustion, we got up.

"Let's go look at the clubs!" I proposed.

"Yeah, let's do it!" Lia agreed.

"I'm ready," answered Rose.

We left Class 1-A.

The three of us knew almost nothing about Thousand Blade Academy's student organizations, so we decided to do a full lap of all the offerings first. We started with the Cheerleading Club, which was stationed right in front of the main building.

"Let's fight, fight, get it done! TBA is number one!"

The girls were each chanting with strong voices that they projected from the bottom of their stomach, and their routine was perfectly coordinated. I was sure that it was the result of hard practice. The performance was so good that it instinctively made me want to start clapping my hands and cheering with them.

One thing worried me about this club, though—the amount of skin they were showing. Their outfits were extremely daring, liberally exposing their backs and legs. Staring at them made me feel more than a little awkward.

"I'm not sure about this club. Those outfits are a little much...," noted Lia, shaking her head. She definitely would have been embarrassed wearing those.

"You think so? They look cute to me," Rose disagreed. She didn't mind the skimpiness.

Oh yeah, her personal clothes were a little showy...

When I'd met her at the Sword Fighting Festival, she'd been wearing a top that completely bared her midriff up to her lower chest, and black athletic shorts.

Her outfit was so revealing that I was afraid to look at her.

Next, we checked out the Swimming Club. There was an outdoor pool on campus with seven twenty-five-meter lanes. It was a meter deep at its most shallow, and over five meters at its deepest. The pamphlet we received when we first joined the academy said that it was used for a variety of activities, from snorkeling to water weight training.

"Hmm... I used to race Ol' Bamboo in the river at Goza Village all the time," I reminisced.

There was a large river near Goza Village with water so clear that you could see the bottom. During the summer, I would often swim there with everyone from the village. Every once in a while, I would also go fishing with Mom to catch the river's delicious bounties.

"The Swimming Club sounds fun!"

"Yeah, it might be nice."

The organization made a good impression on both Lia and Rose. After watching its members swim for a little while, we decided to move on. We continued to observe a variety of clubs until we arrived at the final one, which happened to be the one I was most interested in—the Swordcraft Club.

"Th-there are so many people..."

The gymnasium, which was where the Swordcraft Club met, was packed with over one hundred members, all intently swinging their blades. They boasted a higher number of participants than any group we'd seen so far.

"Hah! Hiyah! Hah!"

The students shouted and swung their swords together at a predetermined rhythm.

"Next, triple strike!" one person called out.

"""Okay!""" everyone else responded.

A giant drum in the middle of the gym was used to tell everyone to move on to a different technique.

"I don't know about this..."

"Yeah, it's a little..."

"A little stiff."

Just as Rose had pointed out, this club had a rigid formality to it.

I want swordcraft to be free and fun.

I didn't need the Swordcraft Club or a predetermined practice schedule to get me to work at the blade. I practiced simply for its own sake, and because I wanted to get stronger. It felt like their thinking and approach to swordcraft differed slightly from mine.

"Want to return to the classroom for now?" I suggested.

"Yeah, let's take some time to think about it," answered Lia.

"Sure," responded Rose.

They both nodded in agreement.

After finishing our observation of all the clubs, we started to head back to our classroom.

"Wait, are you Allen?!"

Suddenly, someone called out to me from behind. I turned around to see who it was.

"Hey, it *is* you! I'm happy to see you took an interest in the Swordcraft Club! Whaddaya think of our practice routine?"

The female student who'd been beating the giant drum ran over to me with shining eyes.

"Uh, well…"

I couldn't tell her to her face that it wasn't the right fit for me.

"Whoops, I haven't introduced myself! I'm Sirtie Rosette, the vice president of the Swordcraft Club. Nice to meet you, Allen!"

Sirtie was an energetic upperclassman with short, light-brown hair, big and beautiful eyes, and healthy, slightly tanned skin. Her protruding tooth gave her a bit of a wild feel.

"I'm Allen from Class 1-A. Nice to meet you, too."

I bowed slightly, and Sirtie grabbed my right hand.

"Wow, look at your hand! How long do you have to practice with the blade to end up with a mitt like this?"

She stared at my blister-hardened palm in wonder.

"U-um…well, I've been practicing since I was five."

"Wow, that's around the same as me! But how'd yours get like this after just ten years?"

"Ah-ha-ha...I've put in a lot of effort."

It was actually ten years plus another billion, but saying that would have led to too many questions, so I laughed and shrugged off her query.

"You're good, Allen! I knew I would like you! Do you have any time right now? How about a practice match?" she offered.

"S-sorry, I have plans for today...," I answered, politely turning her down.

I needed to converse with Lia and Rose about what clubs they liked. Although I felt bad about turning Sirtie's invitation down, I really didn't have time for a duel.

"...So, Allen, wanna get some sparring in?"

She asked nearly the exact same question, her smile never leaving her face.

"No, I—I really don't have time—"

I tried to refuse more clearly, but Sirtie interrupted me by snapping her fingers. The next moment, some members of the Swordcraft Club stood in front of the entrance to the gymnasium to block my escape.

"Wh-what?"

"Sorry, Allen, but I can't let you slip away. It's not easy to come by a talent like you!" she insisted with a fiendish smile.

Haah...

I sighed internally. I'd been dragged into yet another fight I wanted no part of.

■

Sirtie beamed as I resigned myself to sparring.

"You'll be fine, Allen! I won't use my Soul Attire in this match!"

"...Thanks."

That actually wasn't what I wanted to say, but...well, whatever.

I need to think positively.

You didn't get an opportunity to cross blades with the vice president of the Swordcraft Club every day. This would definitely be a good experience.

Sirtie isn't going to listen to a word I say anyway...

The fastest way to get a handle on this situation was going to be dueling her.

"I'm good in this martial-art uniform, but what about you, Allen? Do you wanna change into one of these? Or are you okay with those clothes?"

"I'm fine with my uniform."

The Thousand Blade uniform was very elastic, and much easier to move in than those martial-art uniforms. She must have been aware of that.

"Got it. Here, take this!" she said, handing me a wooden sword used for training.

"Thank you."

As soon as we readied ourselves, the student acting as the referee raised his voice.

"This is a practice match between Sirtie Rosette and Allen Rodol! Both contestants, please move to the center of the gym!"

Sirtie and I walked where we were told.

"Are you two ready? On my mark...begin!"

We both adopted the middle stance as soon as the match began.

"..."

"..."

We stood in silence, observing each other. I analyzed her build and demeanor to try to deduce her style of combat.

I can tell through her uniform that her legs are quite developed... She must be pretty agile. I need to watch out for her thrusts.

One other thing caught my attention.

Her center of gravity is a little farther back than average.

She most likely fought with a defensive style. I guessed that she would focus on blocking and aim for counters. Once I finished my general analysis, I called out to her.

"Are you not going to come at me, Sirtie?"

"Ha-ha, it would be unbefitting of me as your upperclassman to be the aggressor. I'm giving you the first move."

"I see. I'll take you up on that. First Style—Flying Shadow!"

Without taking one step toward her, I released a projectile slash attack from a distance where she wouldn't be able to counter. She laughed fearlessly in response.

"I was ready for that!"

Sirtie had probably watched my matches at the Elite Five Holy Festival, so she calmly deflected the approaching Flying Shadow. However, that was exactly what I'd expected her to do.

"That was a distraction," I announced.

"?!"

I had hidden behind the Flying Shadow as it approached her, and then I slipped behind her.

"Eighth Style—Eight-Span Crow!"

"O-Open Circle Style—Circle of Wind!"

She spun her wooden sword to trace a circle and deflected all eight of the approaching slices. Not only were her movements polished, but she also used her sword almost like a staff.

"You caught me slightly off guard, but you'll need to do better than that! You won't break through my Open Circle School of Swordcraft with a move that toothless!"

"Apparently..."

The Open Circle School of Swordcraft was incredible. I never would have expected her to counter so perfectly from such a disadvantageous position. This style obviously specialized in defense.

This just got a little interesting!

All the opponents I'd crossed blades with until now, Dodriel and Shido included, had fought offensively. This was the first time I'd encountered an opponent like Sirtie, who used her sword defensively.

"Time to get serious!" I shouted.

"Ha-ha! Bring it on!" she responded.

I approached her with a single step, then struck at her with an ordinary swing. I didn't use moves from any Schools of Swordcraft. Downward diagonal slices, vertical slashes, thrusts—I hounded her with only the most fundamental of techniques.

Our first interaction clearly showed me that moves like Eight-Span Crow that release multiple slashes at once won't work against the Open Circle Style.

She would just deflect them with Circle of Wind again. With that in mind, I needed to flourish my weapon faster, heavier, and sharper than usual. I needed to keep pressing her with well-honed attacks!

"Haaaaaaaah!"

"Huh?! Y-you're so fast!"

Sirtie's guard steadily crumbled against my relentless chains of blows, and before long, a chance to break through her guard finally manifested.

"Take this!"

I executed a carefully aimed thrust.

"Wha—?! ...Almost got me."

However, she just barely deflected it with her wooden sword.

Shoot, that was close...

If my thrust had been less than half a second faster, I would have undoubtedly connected with her shoulder.

I'll get her next time. I will break her defense!

I then took a forward-bent posture, and Sirtie told me to stop.

"W-wait, Allen...did you go easy on him in that duel?!"

I assumed she was referring to my duel with Shido.

"No, I always go all-out."

A duel between sword wielders was serious business. I would never go easy on someone.

"R-really? I feel like you've gotten so much faster since then, though!"

"You think so? I'm happy to hear that."

It genuinely delighted me to have other people acknowledge my growth. I felt a renewed desire to work even harder.

"I don't have much time, so I'm gonna continue the match, okay?" I announced.

"..."

I slid half a step toward her, and she dropped her center of gravity to assume a perfect defense.

...Thank goodness.

If she was going to emphasize her guard that much, I wouldn't need to worry about counters anymore. That meant I could put even more energy into my blows!

"Haaah!"

I rushed forward and swung my weapon down.

"Grrr..."

Sirtie stopped my wooden blade with hers. Now that there was no threat of a counter, I struck relentlessly, pushing her much harder than I had before.

"Haaaaaah!"

"A-Allen, stop! Stop, stop, stop!" Sirtie shouted repeatedly, maneuvering desperately to hold off my blade.

"What is it?" I asked without letting up one iota.

"S-stop, please! Can you give me some time to think? I need a quick time-out!"

"A-a time-out?"

If this had been a duel, I would have rejected her outright. This was a practice match, though, so...whatever.

"Haah, fine. Make it quick, though."

"Th-thanks! I appreciate it, Allen!"

Sirtie took one, two, three steps back from me. What she didn't know was that this was the worst mistake she could have possibly made.

"Sirtie, no!"

"Huh...? Bwah!"

She walked backward into one of the Hazy Moons I had set while we were sparring. It nailed her right on the back of the head.

"Wha...?"

The harsh blow took her completely by surprise. Her eyes rolled back, and she collapsed.

T-talk about unlucky.

I'd only set three Hazy Moons throughout the entire expanse of the gymnasium.

She didn't even need to move away from me like that...

I stood there dumbfounded as I examined my fainted opponent.

"S-Sirtie?! What the hell just happened?!"

"A slash hit her! Look closely; there are others set throughout the gym!"

"S-someone get a stretcher, now!"

Some members of the Swordcraft Club rushed in to pick her up.

"V-victory goes to Allen Rodol!"

As the gym descended into panic, the referee loudly declared the result of the practice match.

"So do you want to return to the classroom?" I asked.

"Y-yeah. Let's just...pretend that didn't happen," Lia responded.

"That was kind of a disaster," said Rose, sighing.

Then while watching Sirtie be carried off to the infirmary, we went ahead and left.

■

"Phew..."

Once we'd reached the classroom, I was finally able to catch my breath.

"Good job, Allen. That must've been exhausting," said Lia.

"She really forced you into that practice match," remarked Rose.

"Ah-ha-ha, yeah. But it did end up being a good experience," I responded.

I felt like I now had somewhat of a handle on breaking through defensive fighting styles.

After making a little small talk, we finally moved on to the main discussion—the club we would join.

"Which one are you going to pick, Allen?" asked Lia.

"I'm curious, too," added Rose.

They both looked at me intently.

"Hmm…"

I thought back on all the student groups we saw while walking around.

"…I'm not going to join any of them."

That was what I'd decided.

"So…you're just going to be club-less?" Lia asked, looking confused.

"Yeah, I don't see any reason to force myself into one," I admitted.

I wanted to experience my student life to the fullest by signing up for a student organization, but…unfortunately, none of them jumped out at me.

And the only one I was interested in, the Swordcraft Club, didn't feel right, either.

Since that was the case, I thought it might be preferable to just not join any of them.

"I see…"

"That's a shame…"

For some reason, Lia and Rose both drooped their shoulders.

"…"

"…"

"…"

An awkward silence fell between us as they sat there with gloomy expressions.

Uh…is this my fault?

I tried to come up with a new topic to break the uncomfortable silence, but Lia spoke up first.

"Oh yeah! What if you started a new group instead?!"

"That's a great idea, Lia!"

Rose immediately agreed with Lia's out-of-the-blue proposal.

"Y-you want me to create a club?"

"Yeah! You just want to swing your sword, right?"

"S-sure, but…"

She wasn't wrong, but her wording made it sound as though swinging my blade was the only thing I had any interest in…

"Then you should go ahead and form a group where all you do is practice swings!"

Lia raised a finger as if to say, *Great idea, right?*

"If it gets recognized as a club, you'll get a certain amount of free access to the academy grounds, and you'll also receive a budget!" she continued.

"Hmm…"

I honestly didn't care about a budget, but having some level of free access to the campus grounds was very attractive.

I wonder if I could even use the pool if I requested it.

Swinging my weapon and performing exercises with water resistance would certainly expand the breadth of my training.

"That does sound nice," I said.

"Right? I'll join, of course!" exclaimed Lia.

"Count me in, too," added Rose.

"Are you sure about this? We really are going to do nothing but practice swings."

"Yes, I don't mind at all!"

Hooray! I just got an excuse to spend time with Allen for the next three years! Lia thought.

"Yeah, that's exactly what I want!"

Yes, I'll be able to study swordcraft right by Allen's side for three years! Rose thought.

They both nodded with a gleam in their eye. It seemed like they were also starved with a desire to get some swings in. I was overjoyed to feel a real fellowship with them.

"Sounds like a plan! Let's get the paperwork done now!" proposed Lia.

"It's best to move quickly!" concurred Rose.

They both dashed out of the classroom and returned just three minutes later.

"Good news, Allen! Reia told us she would be our adviser!" Lia announced.

She was grasping a paper titled *New-Club Application* in her right hand.

"You need at least three people to be recognized as a student group. That's perfect," added Rose.

She had a pamphlet titled *General Club Rules* in her left hand.

"I-I see...thanks."

I hadn't yet gotten up from my desk, but things were moving along quite quickly.

Lia then filled out the required fields in the New-Club Application form, and Rose carefully read the General Club Rules pamphlet.

"That does it! All we have left is the name. Have anything in mind, Allen?" Lia asked.

"You're the president, so you should decide," said Rose.

Since when did I become the club president?

"Hmm... Let's keep it simple. How about the Practice-Swing Club?" I suggested.

I went for a simple name that clearly described what we would be doing.

"*Practice-Swing Club...* I like it!" Lia answered.

"No objection here. Simplicity is best," agreed Rose.

As we took care of the paperwork, our classmates streamed back into the room, having finished touring the extracurricular offerings.

"Hey, what're you up to, Allen?"

"Does that say *Practice-Swing Club*? Are you starting an organization of your own?"

"Wait, Allen's starting a club?! Sign me up!"

"C-count me in, too!"

"Hey, Allen, I'm planning on becoming a member of the Swimming Club. Do you mind if I join both?"

Once I gave the okay for people to participate in other clubs in addition to mine, the entire class signed up for my group.

And thus, the Practice-Swing Club ballooned to thirty members immediately after its creation, which was certainly unusual for a brand-new association. It didn't take long for us to build up a reputation throughout the academy as "that group of weirdos who swing their swords in silence every day in the recesses of campus."

■

Once we'd finished another day of strict Soul Attire lessons, I returned to our classroom for afternoon homeroom. Chairwoman Reia performed her usual end-of-day address at her podium.

"I think that covers it for today. Oh yeah, the Club-Budget War is next week. All participating students should come ready to compete!"

""""Yes, ma'am!""""

"That's all for now. You're dismissed!"

The chairwoman left the classroom.

"...Club-Budget War?" I wondered aloud.

Everyone else seemed to be aware of it, but I was fairly ignorant about Thousand Blade and the Elite Five Academies, so I had no idea what it was.

Was that written in the pamphlet? I pondered while gathering my things.

"The Club-Budget War is almost here, Allen!"

"It's gonna be intense!"

Lia and Rose hounded me excitedly.

"Sorry, I don't actually know what that is…," I admitted.

"Really?!" Lia responded, surprised.

"It's one of the signature events of the year at each of the Elite Five Academies. It's pretty famous," explained Rose.

"I-it's famous? Could you tell me about it?" I asked.

Lia obliged.

"The Club-Budget War is a competition that all student groups with a membership of ten or more people are required to participate in!"

Calling that a war sounded like an exaggeration.

"Each association picks three members, and they compete for the top club budget in the academy! The matches are one-on-one sword duels, of course!"

"I—I see…"

So essentially, it was a sword tournament with a club budget riding on it.

"Look at this," Rose said.

She showed me a bundle of papers with the heading *Club Budget-War Guidelines*. They contained detailed rules for the event, as well as the budget multiplier that clubs would receive based on their finishing position.

Sixteenth place and lower all received the same funding. Eighth place through fifth place had their budget quadrupled. Third place had their budget multiplied by sixteen, second place had their budget multiplied by thirty-two, and incredibly, first place had their budget multiplied by sixty-four.

"First place receives sixty-four times more budget than sixteenth place and lower… This is a really big deal," I observed.

"That's right. If a large group like the Swordcraft Club were to place below sixteenth, it would be a disaster for them," Rose added.

"Yeah, it would…"

They needed funding for equipment like wooden swords and armor, consumables like medicine and bandages, travel expenses, and more. To cover all these fees, they would have to aim for a high finishing place.

Lia continued her explanation.

"The three participants from each group must include a first-year. The Student Council doesn't have that restriction because of their small size, but they're the exception to the rule. It's not an exaggeration to say the Club-Budget War is *the* reason that student associations put such a fierce effort into Recruiting!"

"Oh, so that's why the upperclassmen have been going so crazy."

I finally understood why they were in such a frenzy to recruit first-years.

Skimming through the Club Budget-War Guidelines bundle, I found two stipulations that caught my eye.

The use of Soul Attire is prohibited in matches involving first-years.

That rule must have been implemented out of consideration for first-years who couldn't yet produce Soul Attire. This would give them a chance.

The other thing that caught my attention was that this wasn't a knock-out competition. Teams were composed of a first, a second, and a captain, just like in the Holy Festival, but unlike that tournament, the winner of the first match did not advance to fight the other team's second.

The first only fought the other team's first, the second only fought the other team's second, and the final match was a showdown between each team's captain. The first team to secure two victories won the round. The rules were very simple.

"Do we really need a budget, though? We're just the Practice-Swing Club."

All we required for our activities were swords and good health. I couldn't imagine we would use too much money. Actually, I doubted we needed any at all.

"It's always helpful to have as high a budget as possible. For example...we could use it to purchase the rights to use school grounds!" suggested Lia.

"We can do that?"

"Yeah. We could negotiate with the Swimming Club or the Swordcraft Club and give up a certain amount of our funds in order to borrow the pool or the gym."

"Wow, that would be really nice!"

On second thought, it sounded like having a higher budget could really come in handy.

We then approached the other members—everyone in Class 1-A—to discuss who would participate in the competition. However, Tessa and the majority of our classmates had already registered to fight for other groups.

Guess I should've expected that.

Students at Thousand Blade Academy were placed into Class A through F depending on their ability with the sword. At least one first-year had to compete for each club. Since Soul Attire was forbidden in matches involving first-years, and because Class 1-A students were the most skilled of their grade, they were going to be in high demand.

As a result, the participants for the Practice-Swing Club ended up being none other than Lia, Rose, and me.

"The three of us are together again," I said.

"Hmm-hmm, let's win the whole thing!" beamed Lia.

"I'd never aim for anything less!" proclaimed Rose.

■

One week later, the Club-Budget War finally arrived. The event was held in Thousand Blade's underground practice facility. A square stage surrounded by spectator seats had been set up in the middle of the room. This was where I'd fought Lia on the first day of school.

A great number of students filled the seats, and the place was abuzz with anticipation.

I didn't expect us to make it this far.

Our first match had been against the Mountaineering Club, our second had been against the Cheerleading Club, our third had been against the Arm-Wrestling Club, and our fourth had been against the Judo Club. We defeated them all and advanced to the championship round.

"We're doing amazingly!" Lia exclaimed.

"This is really impressive for our first tournament," Rose concurred.

They both examined the bracket.

"M-man, you two are good...," I said.

I hadn't gotten to fight once on our path to the championship. Lia and Rose, whom we positioned as the first and second respectively, had taken every round so far in just two bouts.

I don't think anyone expected a team of only first-years.

Soul Attire was not allowed in these matches, so the upperclassmen who'd participated hadn't been able to duel according to plan, and they'd lost one after another.

"The championship round is about to begin! I'm sure you all are aware of this already, but just in case, I'm going to explain the special rule of this final round!"

The female student serving as the announcer began commentating with a loud, well-projected voice.

"Up until now, in sweeps—a single team claiming victory in both the first and second rounds of a match—the captain did not participate. In the championship bout, however, the captains go up against each other regardless of whether the round was already decided in the first two matches! I ask that our final contestants put their skills on display and set an example for each and every student with an excellent championship duel!"

She paused to take a breath, then continued in her booming voice.

"Now, it's time to introduce the participants on each team! First, we have the total weirdos who swing their swords nonstop all over campus! They're the dark horse of this year's Club-Budget War—the Practice-Swing Club! Their first is the Black and White Princess, Lia Vesteria! Their second is the Bounty Hunter, Rose Valencia! Their captain is Thousand Blade Academy's number one troublemaker, Allen Rodol!"

"Total weirdos"? She didn't have to introduce us like that.

Also, where did that title that she gave me come from?

The three of us walked up onto the stage.

"Let's go, Allen, Lia, and Rose! You can do it!"

"You've got this! We're cheering for you!"

"It'd be a waste not to win it all now!"

We received loud cheers from a section of the crowd. I looked toward it and saw our classmates waving at us.

"On the other side, we have the behind-the-scenes rulers of Thousand Blade—the Student Council! Their first is the secretary, Lilim Chorine! Their second is their treasurer, Tirith Magdarote! Their captain is none other than our Student Council president, Shii Arkstoria! Let's see…according to my information, their notorious vice president is currently out of the country due to a 'penalty game' and, thus, is absent for the Club-Budget War!"

Our opponents were all girls whom I'd seen around campus many times. If memory served, every one of them were second years. There were only four members in the Student Council, so unlike the other clubs, they were not required to put forward a first-year. That was written in the Club Budget-War Guidelines.

Did she say the vice president is out of the country due to losing a penalty game?

That sounded like a harsh punishment. Just what kind of game had they been playing?

"Without further ado, let's get the first match started!"

The championship round between the Practice-Swing Club and the Student Council was about to begin.

■

The first two matches of the championship round were close, but we ended up losing both of them.

"…They're really strong."

I was referring to Secretary Lilim Chorine, and Treasurer Tirith Magdarote. Lia and Rose had been undefeated until now, but they fell one step short of winning us the championship.

"I-I'm so sorry, Allen…," Lia apologized.

"Damn… Sorry, I'm ashamed," said Rose.

They both drooped their shoulders, regret etched on their faces.

"Don't worry about it. I'm just glad neither of you got hurt."

I glanced behind me at the other team.

"I knew you could do it, Lilim and Tirith! That gives us the championship!"

"Victory was ours for the taking!"

"They were stronger than I expected, though. Are they really first-years? I'm tempted to believe they're lying about their age…"

The members of the Student Council joyfully exchanged high fives.

"The Practice-Swing Club has already been eliminated due to the Student Council's victories in the first two matches, but as I said earlier, we're going to go ahead with the final match anyway! It's time for the captains to duke it out!"

The announcer resumed her commentary, and the crowd revved back up.

"Let's get this started! On one side, we have the captain of the Practice-Swing Club! He overpowered Ice King Academy's wonder boy at the Elite Five Holy Festival but was disqualified and suspended for unruly behavior! He's Thousand Blade Academy's number one problem child—Allen Rodol!"

Hmm... She hadn't said anything fallacious, but she also didn't have to go out of her way to make me sound so bad.

"Facing him, we have the mega prodigy who rose to the top of the student body in her second year! She's your Student Council president—Shii Arkstoria!"

Shii had beautiful black hair that fell down to her back, skin as white as snow, and large, gentle eyes. I guessed she was around 163 centimeters tall. She had a very sweet face; she totally projected *big sister* vibes.

"Hee-hee, don't go too hard on me, Allen," she teased, holding out her right hand.

"Let's have a good match, President," I responded.

We exchanged a firm handshake.

She's the leader of the two students who defeated Lia and Rose.

Shii was undoubtedly more skilled than me. I couldn't let myself forget that.

The announcer spoke up again as soon as we took our positions at the center of the stage.

"Are you both ready? The captain match starts on my mark... Begin!"

I sprang to action as soon as she gave the signal.

"First Style—Flying Shadow!"

I hurled a giant projectile slash attack toward her, then approached her while hiding behind it. This was one of my best moves, and it was very difficult to deal with your first time against it.

"Moves that obstruct your opponent's vision are best used as diversions, Allen."

"Wha—?!"

The president calmly deflected the Flying Shadow and fixed her gaze on me.

Sh-she saw through me?!

"C-Cloudy Sky Style—Cirrocumulus Cloud!"

On a split-second decision, I fired four simultaneous slash attacks. It was a move I used for deception.

"Oh, Allen, four just isn't going to cut it."

She dodged two of the slashes gracefully, then easily deflected the other two. Her composure, vision, and swordcraft were all at a very high level.

She's so strong. And unlike Shido, her strength stems entirely from her skill.

It was clear that superficial blows weren't going to work against her.

"You're not the president for nothing...but can you deal with this? Cherry Blossom Blade Secret Technique—Mirror Sakura Slash!"

I brought down four mirrored arcs from the left and right, making eight in total.

"Ooh, that's beautiful! But still not good enough."

She deflected all eight slashes faster than I could blink, without even using a move from a School of Swordcraft.

A-amazing...

I didn't expect for a second that she would deal with Mirror Sakura Slash so perfectly. She clearly outclassed me in pure technique.

But I still have a card up my sleeve!

The attack that I'd used to cut through the World of Time and defeat Dodriel's Shadow Sovereign!

"Fifth Style—World Render!"

This was the strongest tool in my arsenal, so powerful that it could slice through the fabric of a world.

"Wow, what an amazing move!"

But Shii dodged it effortlessly.

"...?!"

"The swing takes too long, though. No matter how mighty an attack is, it means nothing if you don't connect."

She'd easily deduced World Render's biggest drawback. Just as she said, the technique was sensationally strong, but it was slow.

...*I'm speechless.*

She was so disciplined with the sword that I couldn't find the words to praise her.

"Hmm-hmm. Come here, Allen."

Shii wore an expression that made it look as though she were beckoning a small child.

"Oooohhhhh!"

I swung at her again and again for a while, but she dodged, parried, and deflected every strike. Not one of my blows connected.

The swordcraft I'd spent so much time honing was completely ineffective against her. The extent of my skill was being made abundantly clear.

Pfft, ah-ha, ah-ha-ha-ha-ha!

It was thrilling to realize that I still had lots of room to grow. And so was flourishing my blade at full strength and squaring off against an opponent I couldn't defeat no matter how hard I tried.

Ahhh, this is a blast... This is really goddamn fun*!*

At that moment—just for that teensy little moment—an enormous wave of power swelled through my body.

"Graaaah!"

"...Huh?"

The next instant, I delivered a ferociously strong, world-shattering maneuver that couldn't have possibly come from me. Shii's sword happened to be in place to deflect it, but she was unable to hold off the absurd strength, so it snapped in two.

""...?!""

The president and I sucked in our breath at the same time. Although I'd performed a completely ordinary horizontal sweep, it had boasted enormous potency.

Did he just emerge for a moment there...?

I put my hand to my chest but didn't feel the stimulation that had occurred when I held a soul-crystal sword.

I must have imagined it...

I looked up to find the her standing there, petrified. She was cradling her broken blade.

"Um...what should we do?" I asked.

Personally, I wanted her to grab a new weapon so we could keep going.

"..."

A scowl flashed across her face, and she shook her head.

"I can't deal with that. I surrender."

"Shii Arkstoria withdraws! The bout goes to Allen Rodol!"

The referee declared the winner of the match, and the crowd went wild.

"Who knew Allen Rodol was packing that kind of punch?! I can't believe my eyes! What a stunning upset! The Student Council president has lost!"

The announcer's commentary incited the crowd to grow even louder.

The Club-Budget War came to an end, with the top budget going to the Student Council, the second highest going to the Practice-Swing Club, and the third highest going to the Judo Club. The Practice-Swing Club received thunderous applause from our upperclassmen and fellow first-years for the impressive feat of finishing second place in our first few weeks of existence.

I'd never been the object of adulation from so many people, and it made me genuinely happy.

I'm worried about her, though...

The president was glaring daggers at me.

Haah...I really don't want any trouble...
Sighing internally, I pretended to not notice her.

◼

It was the day after the Club-Budget War. I was eating lunch together with Lia and Rose as per usual when an announcement was broadcast throughout the school.

"Allen Rodol of Class 1-A, please report to the Student Council room immediately. Allen Rodol of Class 1-A..."

That was undoubtedly the voice of the Student Council president, whom I'd clashed with the day before.

It was as clear as day that this wasn't an important matter, but...I couldn't ignore summonses that were made over the intercom.

Thus, I dragged my feet to the Student Council room.

◼

"So, Allen."

"What is it, President?"

Shii began bombarding me with questions as soon as I reached the Student Council room, all the while wearing a terrifying smile on her face. Four people were there in total—me, the Student Council president, Secretary Lilim, and Treasurer Tirith. Lilim was sharpening her sword, and Tirith was snacking on sweets while engrossed in a fashion magazine. Neither of them showed any intention of calming their leader down.

"Can you tell me exactly what that was yesterday?" Shii asked from her elegant chair. I was standing on the other side of her desk.

"What are you talking about?"

"Playing dumb, are we? Then I'll reword the question. Were you going easy on me at first?"

"No, not at all."

I'd fought my hardest for the entirety of our match.

She slammed her hands on the desk and stood up.

"You liar! How do you explain that last attack, then? How did you break my sword?!"

"Um, well…"

Honestly, even I still didn't know what that had been.

I don't think he *had anything to do with it…probably…*

What I'd felt the previous day hadn't been quite the same as the odd sensation from when my Spirit Core had possessed my body. The chief difference between the two was that I hadn't perceived any stimulation in my soul.

"It must have been great staging that dramatic reversal after I dominated the entire match. You embarrassed me in front of the whole academy!"

"I was only trying to win…"

The president may have looked like the mature, older-sister type from the outside, but on the inside, she seemed a little childish. Steaming, she plumped back down into her chair.

"Do you enjoy bullying girls?"

"N-no, that wasn't my intention at all…"

"…"

"…"

Shii suddenly fell silent. Her glare made me uncomfortable.

"…I see you're not going to apologize."

Apparently, she'd been waiting for me to say sorry. How was I supposed to know that?

"If you're going to be that stubborn about it, then I challenge you to a game."

"A game?"

I wasn't sure what she meant.

"Durrrrrrrrrr…ta-daa!"

She made a horrible drumroll sound with her mouth, then produced a deck of cards from her desk drawer.

"Uh…do you mean a card game?"

"Exactly! Do you know how to play poker, Allen?"

"I know the rules…"

"Good."

She took out twenty coins and handed me ten of them.

"What are these for...?"

"Hmm-hmm, those are your lives."

With a strange smile, she began to explain how it was played.

"We're going to bet these lives on a game of poker. The rules are extremely simple, so feel free to zone out during my explanation if you want."

She paused before continuing:

"We both start by putting one life into the pot. Next, we draw five cards each, and then it's time for the first betting interval. You can either raise the bet or put in the same amount. If your opponent raises the bet, you must match that amount the next turn."

There was nothing particularly unusual about that. Just plain old poker.

"After that, we have one opportunity to exchange cards, and then we'll enter the final betting interval. You can bet extra lives if you have a good hand, or you can fold if you have a bad one."

"What happens if we fold?"

"You lose half of the lives you've bet that round. Decimals are rounded up. If neither of us fold, we'll both show our hands faceup on the table. The person with the best hand wins and takes all the lives bet that round."

Shii finished explaining the general rules.

"Put simply—we're playing ordinary poker, and the first person to hit zero lives loses," she clarified.

"Easy enough," I responded.

Nothing stood out about the rules. You could find this type of poker anywhere.

I should look for a good place to lose on purpose...

She would only continue to pester me if I won this match.

The best way to end this with no ill will would be to lead most of the game and then lose in the end.

Shii then added some stakes that I wanted no part of.

"And the loser must listen to anything the winner says, no matter how ludicrous!"

"...Are you serious, President?"

"As earnest as can be. The loser must comply with *any order* the victor gives. Got it?"

"Okay, fine..."

I could see there was no way she was going to back down. In that case, the best thing to do was to go ahead and start playing.

Fortunately, I'm not bad at cards.

In fact, I was pretty sure I could beat her.

"All right, let's begin our commemorative first game!"

We each placed one life in the center of the table.

"Hee-hee, my heart is pounding," she said.

She picked up the deck and dealt us five cards each.

Oh...she's cheating.

I clued into it as soon as the match began.

She's the kind of person who's childish enough to challenge someone to a competition and then cheat without feeling any sense of guilt...

She *had* ascended to the heights of Student Council president in only her second year—I supposed it shouldn't have been surprising that she would be such a schemer.

This was making me feel nostalgic.

Ol' Bamboo was great at cheating at cards.

When I was young, I would constantly pester him to teach me the tricks of the trade whenever he would spring one of his crooked techniques on me.

I reminisced on old times as we played. Luckily, Shii's cheating was very basic. I had plenty of time to put my plan into action. After the fourth round, my preparation was complete.

That'll do it... Now I just have to wait for her to make her move.

We went through a couple more rounds, taking turns stealing each other's lives. It was a total back-and-forth match. Then when we advanced to the seventh round, she finally made her move.

"What's that look, Allen...? You must have a good hand."

"You're good at this, President. It's like you can read my mind."

I had a pair of twos and a pair of fives in my hand. Furthermore, I hadn't exchanged cards yet, so I had a good chance at a three of a kind or a full house.

"Ha-ha, it's clear on your face."

But it wasn't me she was looking at... She wore a self-satisfied expression, not suspecting for a second that I'd figured out her deceit.

"I don't want this seesaw game to go on forever. What do you say to us both betting it all this round?" she offered.

This was exactly what I expected. As I chuckled internally, I responded with total calm outwardly.

"Ah-ha-ha, you're scaring me, President. You must have some really strong cards."

"Hmm-hmm, I'm sure it's about the same as yours."

"...Okay. I like my hand, too, so I accept your challenge."

"Great. I'm swapping out a card!"

She quickly—too quickly—exchanged a card. The one on top of the deck must have been the key to securing a powerful play.

"Go ahead and switch one if you want, Allen."

The president was beaming; she thought her victory was guaranteed.

"I think I will."

I discarded my entire hand...

"...Huh?"

...then drew five cards from the deck and laid them facedown on the table.

"Y-you replaced your entire hand?!"

"Ah-ha-ha! I like leaving it up to luck in big showdowns like this."

"You haven't even looked at your cards. Are you in your right mind?!"

"Yeah, I'm challenging you with this."

"..."

Shii gulped.

"What are you going to do? You can fold if you want," I proposed.

She could still get out of this by making a tactical retreat. That would allow her to escape defeat by losing only half of her lives.

"Ha…you're not going to fluster me like that!"

Did he mess with the cards? No, that's impossible! I dealt them myself and shuffled them before that. He's had no opportunity to meddle with them. That means this is a guaranteed bluff! thought Shii.

"Really? Darn…"

That was her final chance, and she let it go.

"L-let's show what we've got! I have four of a kind with four eights! Show me what you have!"

"Okay."

I flipped over my five cards one by one.

Ten of spades. Jack of spades. Queen of spades. King of spades.

"No way!"

And the final card was—the ace of spades.

"Sorry, President. I have a royal flush—that gives me the win."

It was four of a kind against a royal flush. I'd won in a landslide.

Lilim and Tirith, who had both been listening in, rushed over to us.

"That's insane! He actually has a royal flush!"

"What are the odds of that, though…?!"

The president looked visibly upset after her unexpected defeat.

"That's way too unlikely! You cheated, you cheated!" she accused, pointing at me with a trembling finger.

"Ah-ha-ha, you're saying *I'm* the one who cheated?"

"…?! What are you insinuating?"

Shii feigned ignorance, so I pointed at one of the cards that was lying facedown.

"These are trick cards. You can tell the number from a pattern on the back."

"…?!"

After I exposed her deception, her face paled as she shut her mouth.

■

The president fell silent for a few seconds after I pointed out her trick cards.

"H-how dare you accuse me of that! Do I look like the kind of person who would pull off such a rotten scheme?!"

Unable to hide her discomposure, she attempted to defend herself again, despite her lengthy pause.

She's still trying to go through with this even after I exposed her ploy... That's some real commitment.

Shii was more stubborn than she looked.

"There's no way out of this, President. I have irrefutable proof."

I directed my gaze to the deck of cards on the desk.

There were small, tightly packed *X*'s printed on the back of the cards moving from the top left to the bottom right. If you looked closely, you could see that one of the *X*'s on each card had a misprint—there was one line missing. You could tell the number on the front of the card by counting from the left to see which *X* had the misprint.

"I'll demonstrate with the card on the top of the deck. Counting from the top left, it's the seventh one. That's the only *X* with a line missing. That means that this is..."

I flipped over the card.

"A seven. See?"

That was exactly what I expected.

"Wow, Allen! I can't believe you saw through Shii's trick cards so easily!" exclaimed Lilim.

"His eye is so good that it's almost creepy...," added Tirith.

They both patted me on the shoulder.

"Grrr..."

No longer trying to counter me, the president chewed her lip. She was finally admitting to her artifice.

"Wh-when did you notice?" she asked.

"From the beginning, of course," I answered.

"Really?!"

"Yes. Ol' Bamboo—er, a gaming expert I know taught me to never trust my opponent's equipment. Which is why I thought to examine the cards, and sure enough...that was how I figured it out."

Ol' Bamboo taught me a lot about typical trick cards and common cheating techniques.

"Even if you noticed the secret of this deck, that doesn't explain the royal flush! How did you do it? I dealt the cards and shuffled them. You never touched them once!" she accused, pointing to the cards in the middle of the desk.

Sh-should I tell her?

It wasn't like Ol' Bamboo ever swore me to secrecy...but revealing his trick felt icky to me.

"Uh, well...I didn't really do anything—"

"You're torturing me, Allen! Please tell me how you did it! I won't be able to sleep tonight!" Shii pleaded, grabbing me across the table.

"T-too close... You're too close, President..."

She was wearing slightly sweet perfume; my pulse quickened a little.

"Come on, Allen! Don't be so stingy! Just tell us!"

"I really want to know, though!"

Lilim and Tirith circled around behind me and gently prodded me in the sides. I was outnumbered three to one, and unlikely to get out without giving them what they wanted.

"Haah...fine. But don't tell anyone, okay?" I caved.

"Thanks, Allen!" said the president.

"Don't worry, I can keep a secret!" assured Lilim.

"I definitely won't tell anyone!" added Tirith.

I began to explain my technique. It honestly wasn't that complicated. I'd just set about collecting the cards I needed at the beginning of the game.

The method was very simple. Whenever it was time for us to show our hands and then return our cards to the deck, I would take any of the ones I needed and hide them in the sleeve of my uniform. I repeated that until I had a royal flush squirreled away.

Then I waited until the right moment to discard my entire hand and simultaneously put my hidden five cards on the top of the deck. This assured that the next five cards I drew would make a royal flush, guaranteeing my victory.

"See? There are plenty of ways to get one over on someone without even touching the cards."

A swindler never expects to get conned themselves. The president had been trying to keep her eyes off the trick cards so that I wouldn't suspect her, which had made gathering the cards I needed a cinch.

"Th-that's despicable, Allen! I never would have taken you for that kind of kid!"

Shii's face went crimson with rage, and she shook me by the shoulders. But she really had no right to take offense; she was the one who'd cheated first.

"Ah-ha-ha, I was pretty sure you would want to win badly enough to cheat."

I'd observed this side of her after our match in the Club-Budget War. She was so upset about her loss that she wouldn't stop glaring at me. Typical behavior from a sore loser.

"Good lord! Are you hearing this, you two? Allen isn't nearly as innocent as he looks!" the president exclaimed.

"I can see that... Behind that gentle facade lurks someone surprisingly tough," agreed Lilim.

"I'm shocked he saw through you the first time, though... That idiot still hasn't noticed after more than a year," said Tirith, sighing.

I guessed they were talking about the vice president, who was currently out of the country due to a penalty game. Shii just kept duping them him with her cards... I felt kind of bad for him.

"We're giving this win to me, right, President?" I asked.

"Urgh..."

She chewed her lip and nodded curtly. Not only had I seen through her ploy, but I had also successfully turned the tables to deceive her—she clearly had no choice but to acknowledge her loss.

"Hmm... Now what kind of order should I give you...?"

Rose had told me that the Student Council president possessed the authority to allot school grounds to clubs, and to hold events like school festivals and Christmas parties. By giving her an order, I could exercise some power over the entire academy.

That said, I don't have any complaints with how things are right now...

Everyone in Class 1-A was a good person, and I was also very satisfied with the courses and facilities.

I can't think of a single thing I want to ask of her.

I struggled to think of how to use this privilege I had no need for.

"H-hey! You're thinking deviant thoughts, aren't you? I can see it on your face! You're going to tell me to do something lewd!"

She was being intentionally nasty to try to embarrass me.

Sigh, I can't believe her...

If she was going to resort to that, I had the perfect response.

"Actually, that's not a bad idea," I muttered.

"...Huh?"

She froze, her eyes wide.

"You said it yourself, President. The loser must comply with any order, *no matter what it is*... Am I wrong?"

"Uh, well, that was just..."

Her face flushed, and she shrank back a step. It seemed like she couldn't handle being pushed around very well.

Geez, Allen is surprisingly aggressive, thought Lilim.

Shii is totally getting played by him... He's skilled..., thought Tirith.

At this point, I thought it best to stop messing with her for what she'd said. Going too far might cause more trouble for me down the line.

"Ah-ha-ha, I'm joking. I wouldn't do anything so terrible," I assured her.

"C-come on, don't bully your senior like that!" she whined.

"Sorry. You were the one who started it, though, so how about we call it even?"

I decided to put this privilege I had gained on hold for now. I figured there might be a time in the distant future when I could use it to my advantage.

"I'm heading out," I announced.

Now that we were done gambling, I started to make my leave.

"W-wait, Allen!" Shii hurriedly called out to me.

"What is it?" I asked.

"Can I ask a favor?"

"A favor?"

She nodded.

"To be honest, I want you to join the Student Council as a clerk."

"Huh? Me?"

"That's right. We've always valued strength above all else. You saw how strong Lilim and Tirith are. I scouted them both personally."

I looked at her fellow council members.

"Ha, I'm sure you saw my match. I'm really something!" bragged Lilim.

"You have no idea how persistent Shii was, though...," added Tirith.

They both reacted differently to what the president had told me.

"I want you to join the Student Council more than anything, Allen... That's why I challenged you to that game."

"Oh, I see..."

She'd been planning on using her command to force me into the Student Council. That was a bit of an overbearing method, but it was very like her.

"Are you going to turn me down...?" she asked timidly.

"What if I used the privilege I just gained to avoid joining the Student Council?"

"You can't do that! That would be way unfair!"

"...Okay."

For someone who tried to come off as a mature upperclassman, Shii was actually quite the opposite. Despite being one year my senior, I couldn't help but think of her as a little kid.

"D-did you just laugh? You laughed at me!" she yelled.

"Must have been your imagination, President," I responded.

I then tried to get our derailed conversation back on track.

"Well, jokes aside...whether or not I should join the Student Council is something that's not up to me."

"It won't get in the way of the Practice-Swing Club at all. We barely have any work that you'd have get done as a clerk. All you would have to do is show up at our regular meeting during lunch."

"...All right. I'll discuss it with my friends and give you my response later. Bye."

Bringing our conversation to a close, I left the Student Council room for real this time.

■

After that, I returned to Class 1-A and told Lia and Rose about what happened with the Student Council.

"Sh-she asked you to join her?! You can't do that!" exclaimed Lia.

"As a member of the Practice-Swing Club, I can't allow her to steal our president," said Rose, seething.

They were way more against it than I would have expected.

"G-got it. I'll go turn her down," I responded meekly.

There was still fifteen minutes left of lunch. Figuring it would be best to go ahead and alert Shii now, I got up from my seat to return to the Student Council room.

"Wait! I'm coming with you!"

"I'll go, too. This is a very important matter."

They were both really fired up about this.

"O-okay, thanks."

I led them both to the Student Council room.

"Here it is," I announced once we arrived.

Lia knocked three times without hesitation and barged in without waiting for a response.

"Excuse me!" yelled Lia.

"Coming in," announced Rose.

Shii, Lilim, and Tirith were playing a friendly game of Tycoon inside the room.

"Ah, you're both from the Practice-Swing Club," noted Shii.

"Hmm... What were your names...?" Lilim wondered aloud.

"The Black and White Princess, Lia Vesteria, and the Bounty Hunter, Rose Valencia. They're both pretty famous...," finished Tirith.

As usual, their reactions were completely different.

"Our Allen is *not* joining the Student Council!" proclaimed Lia.

"We won't let you steal him from us!" shouted Rose.

The president bolted up in response to their forceful assertions.

"Hmm...and why are you so against him accepting my invitation?" she asked.

"Because Allen is our club president!"

"Exactly."

"Hmm, I'm sure you've already heard this from him, but the clerk really wouldn't have any work to do. His joining would have no bearing on the Practice-Swing Club. All that would be required of him is attending our regular meetings at lunch."

"A-Allen does that with us!"

"Sorry, but we won't surrender that time!"

Lia and Rose doubled down.

"Oh...*that's* what this is about."

Shii nodded to herself as if she had come to some realization.

"Then how about this? You two can join the Student Council with him," she offered.

"Huh? Us?"

"The Student Council?"

"That's right. We still have open clerk positions, and considering your strength, you would both be more than welcome. We have a lot of fun here. For instance, we use our massive club budget to throw as many snack parties a month as we want!"

"Snack parties?"

"With Allen?"

The president was swaying them.

"You should be using the budget for the administration of the Student Council...," I objected.

Shii ignored me completely and continued tempting Lia and Rose.

"The Student Council also goes on a lodging trip in the spring and summer. We've decided on a resort in the south for this summer. You'd be able to go to the beach and hold barbecues with Allen. The unforgettable experiences you'll have will naturally bring you closer to him."

"I can go to a resort with Allen…"

"And enjoy the beach and barbecues with him…"

This discussion was getting weird.

Hee-hee, just one more push! thought Shii.

The president approached Lia and Rose and whispered something in their ears.

"Also…you know how boys are. Once you change out of your formal uniforms and show him your assets in a revealing swimsuit…you'll knock him dead."

""…?!""

I had no idea what she'd just told them, but both of their faces flushed red.

"Allen, let's join the Student Council!" exclaimed Lia.

"After some thought, it doesn't sound so bad after all," added Rose.

"…Huh?"

Before I knew it, my two trustworthy blades had joined the Student Council.

"…What did you fill their heads with, President?" I asked.

"That's a secret! I won't tell a naughty kid who cheats at cards!" she answered.

Shii huffed like a child. She still hadn't gotten over our game.

"There's nothing preventing you from entering the Student Council now, Allen! You'll join, right?" she asked.

I looked at Lia and Rose, and they both nodded.

They were dead set against it before. What did Shii say to them?

Well, in any case, Lia and Rose were in favor. Personally, I didn't see any reason to refuse if it didn't take away from my time with the blade.

"Haah…fine. I'll join the Student Council."

"Yay! We got Allen!"

That was the beginning of my double-club life with the Practice-Swing Club and the Student Council.

CHAPTER 4

Unexpected Encounters at Summer Training Camp

It was the day after I joined the Student Council as a clerk. After morning classes, Lia, Rose, and I gathered in front of the Student Council room to attend the regular lunch meeting that they held every day. I knocked for the three of us.

"Come in."

We heard the president's melodic voice.

"Excuse us."

We opened the door to find Shii, Lilim, and Tirith. They were sitting in their usual places with their lunches placed on their desk.

"Welcome, Allen, Lia, and Rose," greeted Shii.

"Today's meeting is very important. I hope you're ready!" Lilim announced.

"All we're doing is eating lunch like usual, though…," Tirith noted.

They had prepared desks for the three of us, and each of them was marked by a plate displaying our name and position. After greeting them quickly, we sat down.

"Let's start with some simple self-introductions!" announced Shii, looking at Lilim to her left.

"Huh? *Ahem.* I'm Lilim Chorine from Class 2-A. I'm the secretary, but only in name. I shove almost all my work onto the vice president! Let's make this semester great!"

Lilim Chorine was an energetic girl with short brown hair, clear skin, and large, distinctive eyes. At about 160 centimeters, she was slightly shorter than the president.

"I'm Tirith Magdarote from Class 2-A. I'm the treasurer, but in name only. I shove all my responsibilities onto that dolt. I hope we can be friends..."

Tirith Magdarote's dark-blue hair stopped just above her shoulders, and her bangs hid her right eye. In total contrast to Lilim, her features gave her serious downer vibes. At 165 centimeters, she was also slightly taller than Shii.

"I'm the Student Council president, Shii Arkstoria, also in Class 2-A. But this, too, is in name only. I entrust all my work to the vice president. I'm looking forward to having fun with you three!"

I was surprised to hear every one of them admit that their positions were just fronts.

Is it okay for them to foist everything on the vice president like that?

Suddenly, Chairwoman Reia and Eighteen's relationship flashed before my mind.

The three of us also performed simple self-introductions.

"I'm Allen Rodol. I accepted the president's invitation to join as a clerk. It's a pleasure to meet you."

"I'm Lia Vesteria. I'm looking forward to getting to know you all over the next year!"

"I'm Rose Valencia. Nice to meet you."

After we finished introducing ourselves, we ate lunch. Shii, Lilim, and Tirith were very good people, so it was a fun time.

One thing was bothering me, though.

These "regular meetings" are just simple lunch gatherings, aren't they...?

Not one thing about Student Council work had come up yet.

...No, I'm probably being too harsh. This is our first meeting together. I bet they're just trying to break the ice.

However, that expectation—that hope—was totally squashed in the end. For the next two-plus weeks, the Student Council truly accomplished nothing whatsoever. They piled important-looking documents from staff meetings, written requests from other clubs, committee reports, and more onto the vice president's desk and left them untouched.

One day, Shii looked at the ever-growing mountain of documents on the vice president's desk and muttered to herself.

"This is getting kind of bad. He's taking much longer to return than I expected…"

If I recalled correctly, the announcer during the Club-Budget War had mentioned that the vice president was out of the country due to a "penalty game." I had been wondering about that for a while, so I seized the moment to ask about it.

"I've heard that the vice president is out of the country, but where did he go?"

Shii's answer was shocking.

"The mineral deposits under the Holy Ronelian Empire."

"…Huh?"

The Holy Ronelian Empire was a corrupt dictatorship ruled by the cruel emperor Barel Ronelia. Liengard prohibited its citizens from traveling there. There was a rumor circulating recently that the Holy Ronelian Empire had created the Black Organization.

"Why did he go somewhere so dangerous?" I asked.

"For excavation."

"For what now?"

"After I won our penalty game, I told him that I wanted a blood diamond, and the vice president said, 'Leave it to me!' and actually ran off to go find one…," Shii revealed with a small sigh.

"He left to get a precious gem just like that?!" I gawked incredulously.

A blood diamond was a very rare mineral, a small amount of which could be mined deep underneath the Holy Ronelian Empire. It shone an intense shade of crimson, and it was beloved by royalty and nobility, owing to its beauty.

However, considering where blood diamonds were found, they

didn't make it to market very often. On the extremely rare occasion they appeared at auctions, they went for eye-popping prices and made the newspaper the next day.

From what I can tell, the vice president seems kind of unhinged.

"Now that I think about it, it's been forever since he left. You don't think he could've...died, do you?" asked Lilim, joining the conversation.

"I can't imagine that imbecile kicking the bucket, though...," Tirith responded.

"Ha-ha, that's true!" laughed Lilim.

It seemed like the incredibly powerful members of the Student Council had complete faith in the vice president's strength.

J-just what kind of person is he...?

I kind of wanted to meet him.

From then on, my days followed the same routine—I attended Soul Attire class in the morning, Student Council meetings at lunch, more Soul Attire class in the afternoon, and then spent all evening with the Practice-Swing Club after school. It was a very fulfilling school experience.

Time flew when you were having fun, and before I knew it, it was June 30—the last day of the first term at Thousand Blade Academy.

"Okay, your answer sheets have been all returned! Anyone with grading mistakes or questions, come to me!" Chairwoman Reia announced, clapping her hands.

We'd taken our end-of-term final the previous day, and Reia had just returned them to us.

"That's about what I expected," I mumbled to myself, looking at the answer sheets I'd just received.

I got a 68 in literature, a 78 in math, a 62 in geography, a 75 in chemistry, and an 85 in military science. I breathed a sigh of relief after seeing that I surpassed the failing mark of 40 on every test. Lia looked relieved as well when she saw my results.

"Good job, Allen! You did it!"

"Yeah, thank goodness."

Students who failed had to take supplementary lessons over summer break, so I was glad to have avoided that.

"Wow. You did as amazing as ever, Lia."

Lia finished with a 90 or higher on all her tests and got a 100 in military science. I had heard that she'd received a privileged education from a young age, but even then, this was an impressive result.

"Hee-hee, thanks."

After confirming that neither of us failed, we both looked toward the person we were worried about—Rose.

She was surprisingly terrible at studying. One day, she'd admitted to Lia and me very seriously that she was "completely lost" with our material. I'd shuddered and told her that she was in serious trouble.

After that, Lia and I had helped Rose study right up until it was time to take the tests.

We did manage to get through everything that would be covered on them...

Despite that, she'd informed us that she felt no different than before she went through all our study sessions, so I was anxious to hear her results.

"How did you do, Rose?" I asked.

"D-did you pass?" asked Lia.

She turned around to face us.

"Ha, I did it!"

Rose proudly showed us her answer sheets; she scored in the 40s on every one of them, barely avoiding failing.

"Hey, good job!"

"That's amazing! You worked really hard!"

"Thanks, guys, I really owe you one..."

We had all avoided failing any exams, which meant we would be able to go on the Student Council's summer training camp.

After the chairwoman finished addressing any grading mistakes and questions, she began the final homeroom of the first term.

"Tomorrow is the day you've been waiting for! The start of summer break!" she announced.

Summer vacation at the Elite Five Academies was a little early compared with other swordcraft academies. It lasted one month, from July 1 to July 31. One of the chief reasons for the length was to give the exhausted first-years a rest from their harsh Soul Attire courses.

"This is your first high school summer vacation. I know you're excited, but don't party too hard! You're dismissed!"

I'd made it through my first semester at Thousand Blade Academy.

■

The next day, I set out into Aurest with a map that Shii had given me. As per usual, Lia and Rose accompanied me.

"How close are we, Allen?" asked Lia.

"Hmm, according to the map, if we turn right here... There it is!"

We rounded the corner to find a large mansion with an expansive courtyard. There was a stone nameplate with the name ARKSTORIA carved into it. Since this was the spot on the map, it had to be the Student Council president's home.

This is a really fancy place...

I stared at the grand, three-story residence.

"Ah, Allen! Over here!"

Shii hopped up and down in the middle of the yard and waved at us enthusiastically. Behind her were two other members of the student council.

"Good morning, President, Lilim, and Tirith," I greeted.

"Morning, Allen," Shii responded.

"Good morning, Allen! It's a beautiful day!" exclaimed Lilim.

"*Yawn...* Mornin'...," said Tirith.

The president and Lilim were their typical selves, but Tirith looked even more listless than usual. Judging from the way she was yawning and rubbing her eyes, she must have been bad in the mornings like Rose. They both looked like they could nod off at any moment.

"What do you think of my casual clothes, Allen?" Shii asked, tugging on my sleeve.

She was wearing a simple white dress. It gave her a slightly more grown-up feel; it suited her.

"It looks great on you," I answered.

"Ha-ha, thanks."

That put her in a fantastic mood, and she hummed as she started to walk toward a building that looked like a storehouse.

"Over here, everyone!"

We followed her into the building, where we found a large aircraft. It looked prepped for takeoff, and I could see three pilots in the cockpit.

"Ta-daa! This is my family's private jet! We're flying it all the way to Veneria Island!"

W-wow...she has a three-story manor and *a private jet.*

They had enough wealth to be mistaken for one of the Five Business Oligarchs living in Drestia.

"Um, are you from a noble family, President?" I asked.

"Hmm, not quite. The Arkstoria family has held important positions in the government for generations. Have you heard of my father, Rodis Arkstoria?"

"Now that you mention it, I have heard that name on the radio a lot..."

I couldn't remember exactly who he was, but I was pretty sure he was a cabinet minister in some government agency.

"Well, that has enabled our family to live in some wealth. There are drawbacks, though," she added, laughing with a grimace on her face. "Moving on...looks like they're ready! Get in, get in!"

"I haven't flown since spring break. I'm excited!" Lilim cheered.

"*Yawn...* I'm excited, too...," Tirith announced drowsily.

The upperclassmen eagerly climbed into the jet, and Lia, Rose, and I followed.

The inside of the jet resembled a luxurious hotel room. It was furnished with a sofa, a bed, and even a kitchen complete with a fridge.

We enjoyed a comfortable flight and arrived at Veneria Island, a resort in the south of the country, in just a few hours. Veneria Island was one of the most popular tourist destinations in Liengard. I had heard that a great number of tourists from the surrounding nations also traveled to the island to bask in its beautiful water and beaches.

When we exited the plane, the sight of the endless sea greeted us.

"Look, Allen, look! It's so pretty!"

"This is beautiful."

Lia's and Rose's eyes lit up in excitement.

"Mmm, the wind is so nice!" exclaimed Shii.

"Echo!!!" shouted Lilim.

"Lilim, you're supposed to shout that on a mountain...," chided Tirith.

The upperclassmen breathed in the Veneria Island air.

I felt a flood of emotion.

This is the ocean...

I'd spent my early years in the inland Goza Village and had dedicated every spare moment in middle school at Grand Swordcraft Academy to swinging my sword. This was my first time witnessing the ocean.

The clear blue water extended as far as the eye could see, the air smelled salty, and the sand was pure white.

It's all just as Mom said!

I was greatly moved at my first glimpse of the sea.

"All right, Lilim, Tirith, and I are gonna go clean up the villa. We haven't used it in a while, so I'm sure it's caked with dust," announced Shii, proposing that we split up.

"We'll help you out!" I offered.

She'd not only treated us to a luxurious flight in a private jet, but she was also even providing us with a place to sleep. The least I could do to pay her back was help with tidying up.

"I-it's okay, we're good! You don't have to do that! We'll handle everything ourselves! It'll take no time at all!" Shii protested, shaking her head emphatically.

"Ah-ha-ha, Shii's saying that 'cause her room is a mess! You wouldn't believe where she puts her under— Brgh!"

The president interrupted Lilim by striking her with a quick, formidable karate chop that knocked her unconscious.

"They say the mouth is the source of all disaster…," Tirith muttered, poking the motionless Lilim.

I could figure out what was really going on from that exchange.

She must have things scattered about that she doesn't want us to see.

The president was cleaning it herself instead of leaving it to a servant. That left no room for doubt.

"…*Ahem*. Anyway! We're gonna go take care of the villa! Hmm… How about you three kill time at the beach shack down that way?" Shii suggested.

"G-got it."

Lia, Rose, and I headed in the direction she'd indicated. After a few minutes of walking on the beautiful sand, a large building came into view ahead of us.

"That has to be it," I said.

"Wow, that place is huge," observed Lia.

"Business must be booming," added Rose.

The beach shack was a large wooden establishment that looked like three ordinary houses joined together. The right half was a shop that sold food like *yakisoba* and curry rice, and the left side featured a great variety of recreational toys, including beach balls and simple inflatable boats.

There's so much to do here. Killing time won't be hard at all.

We wandered around inside the shop, and something caught Lia's attention.

"Watermelon splitting?"

She was looking at a "Watermelon Splitting Set," which contained a watermelon, a stick, and some blindfolds.

"It's a traditional game in this country where you try to split open a watermelon while your vision is obscured," explained Rose.

"I-is it fun?" Lia asked curiously. They must not have played that in Vesteria.

"Ah-ha-ha, it might be nice to try it later," I said.

We continued to enjoy browsing the various goods in the shop until an old man in front of us suddenly stabbed at Lia.

"Lia, get back!" I warned.

"Aaah!" she screamed.

I grabbed her with my right hand, drew my sword with my left, and managed to stop his dagger.

"Shit…you little brat…"

The old man had a mean scowl on his face after failing at his strike.

"That's a cane-sword… Who are you?" I asked.

That wasn't a random assault. He was clearly aiming to assassinate Lia.

"Haah, what did I tell ya? We should've all nailed them at once instead of wasting time on a surprise attack…"

"Princess Lia, I bear no grudge against you, but you die here today."

Every customer in the shop drew a blade, cornering us.

There are forty, no, fifty of them…

Our summer vacation was off to a dangerous start.

■

After the strange group of assailants surrounded us, Rose leaped into action.

"Cherry Blossom Blade Style—Sakura Flash!"

"Huh—? Gwah!"

Rose thrust her sword forward, sending one of the goons flying outside the shop.

"We're at a disadvantage indoors against this many foes! Let's leave this place first!" she commanded, smoothly dashing out of the beach shack.

That's our Rose.

She was probably able to take charge like this because of her experience as a witchblade. Her calm demeanor despite the abrupt nature of the battle was reassuring.

"Let's go, Lia!"

"Okay!"

We slipped through the gap that Rose had opened in their mob and ran outside the shop.

"Hey, stop right there!!!"

Yelling, the seething assailants pursued us.

Once we escaped from the beach shack, we put our backs to one another to cover our blind spots.

"Goddamn kids… Form into assault groups and surround them! Go!"

""""Yes, sir!""""

On one man's orders, the assailants gathered into squads of three.

"Haaaaah!"

"Take this!"

"Dieeeeee!"

They came at us with downward swipes, thrusts, and diagonal slashes. Our attackers took commands well and showed some semblance of swordcraft. They'd clearly studied the blade before. But they were no match for us.

"Eighth Style—Eight-Span Crow!"

"Cherry Blossom Blade Style—Lightning Sakura!"

"Hegemonic Style—Hard Strike!"

They were all unskilled.

"Ga-hah!"

"Gyaaa!"

"S-so strong!"

There was no way that some assailants who had no more than dabbled in swordcraft would stand a chance against prodigies like Lia and Rose, or even the Reject Swordsman.

"You're finished. If you continue to fight, we'll show no mercy," I threatened, pointing my weapon at them.

"C-crap…"

Collapsed on the ground, they gritted their teeth in frustration. In just a few minutes, we'd succeeded in subduing the attackers.

"Rose, tell the beach-shack employees to call the holy knights."

"S-sure."

This was as much as we could do for now. We were better off letting the holy knights question and identify these miscreants.

"Those people... They were after me, weren't they?" Lia mumbled, visibly worried.

"They said 'Princess,' so they probably were," I answered.

Their actions had been well coordinated, so it was possible they were assassins sent by a country with an antagonistic relationship to Vesteria.

The fallen goons then began to speak.

"...I'm using it."

"A-are you insane?!"

"Even if we make it back, we'll be executed for failing our mission! We may as well take the chance!"

I couldn't make sense of what they were saying.

"What are you all talking about...?"

Right after I asked that question, each one of them pulled a blue, glasslike object out of their pocket and tossed it into their mouth.

"Urgh... GAAAAAAHHH!"

"Hagh... Hagh... AAAAAHHHHH!"

They began rolling on the ground and screaming in anguish. Something was obviously wrong with them.

"Wh-what the...?!"

"They all just ingested some kind of pill!"

The three of us backed up to be safe and readied ourselves. The collection of assailants rose slowly, as pale as ghosts.

"Haaah-haaah... Heh-heh-heh... You brats are finished!"

Somehow, every one of them was wielding Soul Attire.

"Th-they can all use Soul Attire?"

"Something's off about them, though..."

Just as Lia noticed, they seemed somehow unhinged.

These Soul Attires all look unstable...

The shape of each of their Soul Attires seemed to morph from one moment to the next. I'd never seen anything like it.

"W-we don't have much time left... Let's end this!" one of the men yelled.

"Urgh... GAAAAAAAAH!"

One of the attackers struck the beach with his large Soul Attire, kicking up a massive amount of sand. The world went white.

""Hiyaaaaah!"""

The men all charged us at once.

"Huh?! How'd they get so fast?!"

They had become so swift that I could hardly believe they were the same people.

"Raaaaaah!"

"Wha—?!"

It wasn't just their speed; their physical prowess had also increased significantly.

Do they all have self-strengthening Soul Attire?

No, that was too unlikely.

"What the heck did you all do?!" I asked.

"Haah... Haah... We took soul-crystal pills... It's a powerful drug that causes your Spirit Core to enter a state of fury and produce a pseudo–Soul Attire..."

"What?!"

Doing something that reckless would place an enormous burden on yourself.

"S-stop right now! Your bodies won't last!" I yelled.

"We know that... That's why you'll die right now!"

They struck at us again and again with blades that literally had their lives riding on them.

"Why are you going so far as to throw your own lives away to kill Lia?!" I asked.

"'Cause His Excellency the Emperor ordered us to eliminate the princess! Haaaaaah!" one of the men screamed, slashing at me diagonally with haphazard might.

"Grrr..."

I defended myself with my sword and then jumped far backward.

"This isn't over yet!!!!"

"Die already!!!!"

"Goddamn brats!!!!"

The assailants yelled as they rushed toward me.

Despite their instability, their Soul Attire granted them enormous power. Their astounding physical strength surpassed human capability. And above all else, they were prepared to give up their lives.

This is bad...

But I had absolutely no intention of losing to opponents who'd abandoned swordcraft entirely to rely on physical prowess and unruly Soul Attire.

"Fifth Style—World Render!"

I decided to meet force with even greater force. Launching an attack that could tear through worlds, I easily overpowered their weapons.

"Ga-hah!"

"T-too strong..."

"S-sacrificing our lives wasn't enough?!"

The ten goons I'd knocked down to the ground groaned, unable to get back up. Their bodies appeared to be past their physical limit.

"Haah... Haah... We can't kill this monster! But we can murder the princess! Everyone, get her!!!!"

One man rallied the others, and the remaining forty assailants charged at Lia simultaneously.

""Huh?!""

This was a death charge with no consideration for their own defense.

Crap...

Clearing away that many people would be difficult even for Fafnir's flames. And regardless of whether she could do it, Lia was far too kind to pull it off. She didn't have it in her to go through with something so unfeeling and cruel.

"Run, Lia!"

"O-okay!"

Remaining composed, she chose to flee.

"Ah!"

A collapsed man near the princess grabbed her ankle.

"Heh, heh-heh… We're gonna finish you off if nothing else!"

"L-let go of me!"

"Lia, look ahead! Defend yourself!" I yelled.

Eyes bloodshot, the criminals were rushing at her from up ahead.

""""HAAAAAAAAH!!!"""" they all yelled.

"Eeeeeeek!" Lia screamed.

""""DIEEEEEE!!!""""

Forty men swung at her with their Soul Attire at once.

"How many people do you creeps need to take down one girl?"

An enormous wall of ice suddenly formed in front of Lia to protect her.

"I-it's hard as steel!"

"Where did this come from?!"

"Is this from someone's Soul Attire?!"

The ice wall was so sturdy that they couldn't even put a crack in it with their overpowered Soul Attire.

"I—I know this skill!"

I opened my eyes wide in astonishment.

"Freezing Spear!"

Giant ice lances appeared in the air and fell like rain.

"GAAAH!"

"It hurts, it hurts!"

"What the hell?!"

An unfeeling and cruel attack that showed no mercy to its targets—I recognized this power, which was so cold that it could turn even a southern resort to midwinter.

"What the hell are you doing struggling against these shrimps, you piece of trash?"

I looked in the direction of the voice to find the ace of Ice King Academy—Shido Jukurius.

"Shido?! What are you doing here?!"

"Huh? Oh, it's you—"

He was interrupted by a beach ball to the temple.

"Shido, put that away!"

"...What was that?!"

For a second, he looked like he was ready to hurt someone, but as soon as he realized that the person who'd thrown the ball was Ice King Academy's chairwoman, Ferris Dorhein, he changed his tone.

"Sorry, madam."

Surprisingly, he put Vanargand away obediently.

"Good grief, did you *have* to go and freeze this nice southern weather...? Wait, you're Allen," Ferris noted.

She was clad in a kimono, as per usual. Trailing behind her were a number of students in Ice King Academy uniforms.

"Hello, Shido and Ferris. What are you all doing here?" I asked.

"We're here for our Student Council's summer training camp," she answered.

"Sh-Shido is in the Student Council?!" I exclaimed in astonishment.

"You got a problem with that?" he spat with a frigid glare.

"N-no...I was just a little surprised."

Shido was aggressive and didn't care for rules. He couldn't seem any less suitable for a position in student government.

"Hee-hee, he's smarter than he looks," Ferris praised, patting him on the head.

"Madam, whaddaya mean 'smarter than I look'...? I don't look stupid," he protested.

"Ha-ha, don't worry. You're adorable just the way you are."

"I'm not cute, either..."

Shido's typically adversarial personality softened before Ferris.

What kind of relationship do they have? I wondered.

"A-are you Lord Allen?!"

A male Ice King Academy student walked toward me, visibly trembling. He had black hair with bangs of moderate length. Tall and slender, he wore black-rimmed glasses. A silver pendant shaped like a cross hung from his neck. I took a second to remember his name.

"Um...your name was Cain, right?"

He widened his eyes in shock.

"Y-you remember me?! I am humbled beyond words. Yes, my name is Cain Material. Ah-ha, I'm in seventh heaven!"

"W-we met only three months ago."

Just a short while had passed since that turbulent Elite Five Holy Festival.

The Holy Festival, our month as witchblades, encountering the Black Organization and dueling Dodriel, the Club-Budget War, our end-of-term tests—thinking back on it, that was a jam-packed three months.

Did Cain act anything like this when I first met him?

I felt like his personality used to be calmer.

"Haah…you've become such a creep," barked Shido, glaring at Cain as if he were a maggot.

"Excuse me, Shido? There's nothing creepy about me! Ah, but never mind that! Master Allen! You're as wonderful in person as I expected you to be! Your demeanor is so dignified! Your body is so well-toned! Your eyes are so full of kindness and strength! The footage can't hope to do you justice!" Cain bellowed, overcome by emotion. His gaze seemed to drink my entire body in.

"Th-thanks…"

There was clearly something wrong with him. His previously cool personality had totally melted away.

"Uh, how did Cain end up like this?" I asked Shido.

"Why the hell would the great Shido have to tell a piece of shit like you? You're the enemy," he answered.

"Y-you're right, sorry…"

I couldn't have picked a worse person to ask. Given how fiercely Shido despised me, there was no way he was going to be amicable and answer my question.

"…"

"…"

An awkward silence fell between us.

"…It happened soon after the Holy Festival," he started slowly.

He's actually answering me…

Despite being dangerous, Shido seemed to have a nice side that came out at surprising moments.

"Cain's grief at his loss to you drove him insane… He said that 'if Allen can overcome a century of imprisonment, then so can I!' and cut his own finger with his Hundred Hellblade."

Hundred Hellblade was Cain's mental-manipulation Soul Attire. Anyone he slashed with his blade had their mind imprisoned in another world for a very brief period of one hundred years. Disappointingly, the world didn't even have a loop feature to allow the target to spend another century there. It was clearly an inferior version of the 100-Million-Year Button.

"People like you, who can endure the Hundred-Year Hell with their monstrous mental fortitude, are few and far between… Cain was transported to the hospital immediately, and when he woke, he was like this."

Shido shook his head in disgust.

"That's exactly it! I was foolish enough to think that I could enter the same domain as God and paid for my mistake by spending a month unconscious in critical condition. However! It was due to my experience that I reawakened! I have not an ounce of regret!" Cain exclaimed.

"I—I see…," I responded.

He had the eyes of a crazy person. I had to watch myself around Ice King Academy students.

"Lord Allen, do you mind if I ask you a question?" groveled Cain.

"No…go ahead."

I didn't want any part of this, but I couldn't just ignore him.

"Thank you so much! I've been dying to know—what did you do during the long one hundred years you spent in that hellish world?"

"Hmm… I mainly just swung my sword."

"Y-your sword?! You swung your sword for one hundred years?!"

"Y-yes."

To be honest, I'd wanted to vary up my training a bit more, but as someone who'd spent over a billion years intently honing my swordcraft, one hundred years felt way too short. As a result, I ended up only having time for practice swings.

"Wow...what incredible mental resilience! What an earnest approach to swordcraft! You really are the greatest, Lord Allen!"

"I'd rather you stop calling me that..."

The Ice King Academy students had been observing me curiously during our conversation. I needed to nip any weird rumors in the bud.

"I—I apologize for my rudeness! I will refer to you as *God* instead!"

"Please, anything but that..."

Cain and I just couldn't seem to get on the same wavelength. The next moment, the sight of a large helicopter hovering in the sky interrupted us. And I couldn't believe what happened next—two people leaped out and began to descend.

""""Huh?!"""""

They landed on the ground after plunging for hundreds of meters.

"Yo, how's it goin', guys?"

"Yes...yes, that would be much appreciated. Uh, yes... Thank you very much."

It was Chairwoman Reia, who looked ready to have a great time, and Eighteen, who was absorbed in a phone call. I had no idea how their legs had managed it, but neither one of them seemed to feel the shock of plummeting to the ground.

"Ch-Chairwoman Reia? And Eighteen, too? What are you doing here?" I asked.

"What do you mean, 'what am I doing here?' How would you make it through the training camp without your adviser's guidance?" the chairwoman responded.

"So you're the Student Council's adviser..."

"Indeed I am! Anyway, we're at a resort! Let's leave our exhausting duties behind and party till we dro— Ferris?! Why are *you* here?!"

The chairwoman's cheerful mood quickly turned to frank displeasure when she saw Ferris.

"That's my line. I was so looking forward to this summer training camp, and now I have to see your ugly mug... Haah, how depressing..."

"What was that, vixen?!"

They started to argue. Those two had been like cats and dogs since their school days.

"Hey, Allen, sorry that took so long... Huh? Who are all these people?"

"Oh, they're from Ice King Academy!"

"Look behind them, though... There's a big group of strange men collapsed on the ground... Something clearly happened here..."

Shii, Lilim, and Tirith had returned from cleaning the villa. Another group arrived at the same time as them.

"This is the Veneria holy knights!"

"The assailants are over there!"

"They've taken heavy injuries... Call the rescue squad!"

It was Rose, leading a large number of holy knights.

"Sorry that took so long. There was no phone in the beach shack, so I went to the nearby station," she explained.

"Okay, thanks for taking the time to do that," I said.

The holy knights worked the scene efficiently. Eventually, one of them strode briskly toward us.

"Those uniforms... Are you all students from Thousand Blade Academy and Ice King Academy? I'd like to ask some questions. Is there a teacher nearby?"

"Um...over there...," I answered, looking toward Chairwoman Reia and Ferris.

"You're one to talk, Crybaby Ferris! Want me to cave your face in like a potato again?!"

"Go ahead and try! I *will* get the upper hand, musclehead!"

The two chairwomen were busy hurling insults at each other. Yikes...this was mortifying.

"Is this a soul-crystal pill?!"

"So the Black Organization was involved in this after all..."

"We need the senior holy knights—contact headquarters!"

They began to move with haste.

"Hey, Shido! Come get some practice swings in with me! It's the word of Lord Allen—of God!"

"Stay back, you four-eyed creep!"

Cain, who had been joyfully practicing slashes, was trying intently to get Shido to join him. Meanwhile...

"I just had a great idea! Why not turn this into a joint summer training camp with Ice King Academy?" suggested Shii.

"Ooh, I like that! That'll motivate everyone for sure!" exclaimed Lilim.

"Oh, come on, you always suggest the most annoying things..."

...I overheard the Student Council president offer up a preposterous idea.

Things got out of hand really quickly here...

After a little discussion, the chairwomen decided that this trip would be made into a joint summer training camp between Thousand Blade Academy and Ice King Academy.

...Please let this end without incident.

While holding that hope in my chest, I let out a small sigh.

■

After the joint summer training camp had been settled on, the members of Thousand Blade Academy went back to Shii's place, and the Ice King Academy students returned to Ferris's villa. We were going to put our luggage away and change.

"Okay, time to head out," I told myself.

Having put on my swimsuit, I headed for the reception room, where we'd agreed to meet. I was wearing a plain black pair of swim trunks and a white parka.

As I waited in the quiet, empty reception room, I thought back to the day's incidents.

What in the world just happened...?

I was especially worried about the attack we'd suffered.

Before we left, the Holy Knights Association's relief squad had arrived and performed first-aid treatment on the heavily injured assailants. The holy knights then arrested all fifty of them, took them to the station, and told Chairwoman Reia and Ferris that they would contact them as soon as they figured out the particulars of the case.

That group was clearly after Lia. They were probably assassins from a country or organization that is hostile toward Vesteria.

Though it was easy to forget about since we were together all the time, Lia was a princess of Vesteria Kingdom. A risk of assassination or abduction always followed her.

I want to help her if I can...

I continued to mull things over as I waited for everyone to change. Eventually, the door in the back right of the room opened.

"S-sorry for the wait..."

"How do I look, Allen?"

Lia and Rose emerged. Lia was blushing and slightly embarrassed, while Rose looked as dignified as ever.

"..."

My breath caught in my throat as soon as I saw them in their swimsuits.

Lia was wearing a halter-neck bikini with a lovely design consisting of white fabric and red frills. What caught my attention more than anything was the way it emphasized her chest... Needless to say, it was quite attractive.

Rose wore a simple black bikini and a thin, black wraparound skirt called a pareu. The black swimsuit contrasted beautifully with her pink-tinged silver hair, and her complexion gave her an attractive air of maturity.

"U-um...you both look good...," I answered, darting my eyes away and answering honestly.

"Th-thanks...," replied Lia.

"Ha-ha, I'm glad you like it," responded Rose.

After I shared my thoughts, we all went quiet.

"""..."""

Lia was glancing at me repeatedly, Rose was standing perfectly still, and I could look neither of them in the eye because of their outfits. An awkward silence that none of us could break fell between us.

Would it be tactful for me to say something?

As I racked my brain for a topic to bring up, a voice cut me off.

"We're here!"

The door in the back left of the room swung open to reveal the three upperclassmen in their swimsuits.

"Hey, Allen, whaddaya you think?" Shii asked.

The president was wearing a white bikini hemmed with blue, and a gray long-sleeved parka over it. The outerwear was open, greatly emphasizing her chest. To my surprise, she was bustier under her clothes than I'd anticipated.

"I—I think it suits you very well," I answered with my eyes downcast.

Beautiful, swimsuit-clad women had surrounded me from all sides. I truly had no idea where to rest my gaze. Shii sensed my discomfort.

"Huh? Is something wrong, Allen?"

Smiling mischievously, she leaned forward deliberately and peered into my face.

"P-President…please stop messing with me," I begged.

"Hmm-hmm, this is revenge for before," she responded with a snort.

She apparently still hadn't gotten over my little prank after cheating at poker.

"Well, everyone's here—let's get going!" she announced.

"Do we not need to wait for Chairwoman Reia?" I asked.

"She already got changed and left."

"R-really?"

I couldn't believe she'd gotten ready faster than me.

"C'mon! Today is the day we put Ice King Academy in their place!" Shii yelled excitedly.

Having finished putting on our swimsuits, we left for Ferris's private beach.

■

After a discussion, Chariwoman Reia and Ferris decided that we would pit Thousand Blade Academy and Ice King Academy against each other in a variety of challenges.

The first match was beach volleyball. Lia and I represented Thousand Blade, while Shido and Cain represented Ice King. Coincidentally, it was a showdown of first-years.

Our match wound up being a fiercely contested, back-and-forth affair.

"You're really good, Shido. I can't believe how much ground you can cover by yourself...," I complimented.

"Give up already, you amateur!" Shido yelled in response.

Lia and I moved together as one, scoring consistently thanks to our great teamwork. As for our opponents, Shido made use of his overwhelming physical might to score by fiercely attacking and blocking. Meanwhile, Cain focused entirely on receiving and passing.

"Allen, here!"

Lia gave me a perfect pass.

"Hah!"

I hit the ball, and it fell barely within the line on the other side.

"Goddamn it!" yelled Shido.

"L-Lord Allen is truly wonderful!" exalted Cain.

The score was now twenty to nineteen. One more point, and victory would be ours.

"Great shot, Allen!" beamed Lia.

"All thanks to your setup!" I responded.

We high-fived.

"God, you guys creep me out... No matter how good your teamwork is, trash is still trash! I'll show you just how superior I am!" Shido exclaimed.

The air around him changed. I felt a brutal, fiendish aura that reminded me of our fight during the Holy Festival.

"Lia, this is match point!"

"Yeah, let's finish this!"

She took a moment to exhale, then spun the ball in the palm of her hand.

"Hah!"

She served skillfully, sending the ball racing with a front spin for the edge of the court.

"Not a chance!"

However, Shido reached it easily with his astounding reflexes.

"Hit it up!" he commanded.

"Okay!" responded Cain.

He put the ball in the perfect position in the center of the court.

"Eat this—Vanar Ball!"

Shido's spike was inhumanly fast, and it seemed to cause the ball to split into four.

"Shoot… Allen, get it!"

It slipped through Lia's block.

"Cloudy Sky Style—Cirrocumulus Cloud!"

My four-part receive blocked the ball before it hit the ground.

"What the—?!" Shido shouted.

Then it traced a high arc and dropped deep within enemy territory.

"Twenty-one to nineteen! Thousand Blade Academy wins!"

The Ice King Academy student acting as the referee loudly announced the result.

"If there are four balls, the only thing you have to do is return all four," I declared.

"You piece of shit…," Shido fumed.

The beach-volleyball match came to an end, resulting in a spectacular victory for Thousand Blade Academy.

"I knew you could do it, Allen! That was amazing!" cheered Lia.

"Thanks, but I couldn't have done it without you," I responded.

Lia and I joyously basked in our victory.

"You were just as breathtaking as I thought you would be, Lord Allen! That was the greatest receive I've ever seen! I was so inspired, I couldn't move a step!" Cain praised me profusely despite being on the opposing team.

"U-uh, thanks…," I responded.

"Which side are you on, you four-eyed freak?!" Shido yelled.

"Ow!"

Shido walloped Cain.

"Hmm-hmm, it seems like we have the superior students this year, Ferris," bragged Chairwoman Reia.

"Grrr...moving on! We're playing beach flag next!" shouted Ferris, quickly announcing the start of the second match.

Beach flag is a staple beach game where the contestants compete to grab a flag that's been placed in the sand twenty meters away. The players start lying facedown and turned away from the flag, and as soon as the whistle blows, they get up and sprint for it. The rules are simple—whoever grabs the flag first wins.

Rose, Shii, and I represented Thousand Blade.

"Getting off to a good start is everything," I said.

"Good thing instantaneity is one of my strengths," stated Rose.

"There's no way we can lose!" exclaimed Shii.

The participants from Ice King Academy were Shido, Cain, and a female student from the Student Council.

"Don't get in my way," warned Shido.

"Wouldn't dream of it," answered Cain.

"Do your best, Shido!" encouraged the female student.

We positioned ourselves facedown on the ground, and then the whistle blew. I stood up and whipped around to witness an astounding sight.

"Ha! You wimps are too slow!"

Shido was already bolting forward and running.

"H-how is he so fast?!"

His reaction time was off the charts. He effortlessly grabbed the flag.

"Ha-ha! My talent is unrivaled!" he boasted with a wicked smile.

He moved so quickly after the whistle, and then he ran like a gazelle. Shido really is on another level, I thought.

That little shit's acceleration is catching up to mine. He's gotten much stronger, too... Is this the influence of that monster? Or is it the result of some gross, boring-as-hell training? Either way, I can't take him lightly, thought Shido.

The evenly matched clash between Thousand Blade and Ice King continued long into the day, eventually settling at a ten-to-ten tie. When Chairwoman Reia and Ferris pushed eagerly for one more bout to settle the score, the competition felt like it would never end.

"This is a joint training camp, so how about we leave it at a tie and finish this at the Royal Sword Festival after summer break?" Shii suggested.

The Student Council president, however, skillfully wrapped things up by guiding their attention to the next major battle. The first day of the joint training camp came to an end, and we headed back to our respective lodges.

■

The first thing we all did after returning to Shii's villa was use its spacious baths to wash off our sweat and exhaustion. Once our minds and bodies were refreshed, we joined back up for a lively dinner.

That was so good...

The meal that the Arkstoria family's personal chef prepared for us could only be described as exquisite. The meat melted in my mouth. The grilled fish was fatty and tasty. The vegetables were so good that I couldn't believe Mother Nature had produced them. I was in heaven.

Currently, it was around ten at night. The members of the Student Council, Lia, Rose, and I were holding a snack party in a fifteen-square-meter traditional-style room that was complete with tatami mats and a low table.

"I think we were around five years old. There was some *crazy* loud thunder, and Shii suddenly started crying!"

"That's so nostalgic! We asked her why she was crying, and she yelped, 'What should we do? The god of thunder is going to steal our belly buttons!' It was really cute, though..."

Lilim and Tirith laughed as they recounted that childhood memory.

"H-hey! Don't tell embarrassing stories like that around those three!" the Student Council president fumed, blushing deep red and bonking the other two on the shoulders.

"Ah-ha-ha, that's adorable," I said, laughing.

"Hmm-hmm, I remember hearing about the god of thunder when I was a little kid," reminisced Lia.

"You were only five; it's understandable that would make you cry," consoled Rose.

While wearing comfortable, loose-fitting *yukata*, we made small talk and indulged in the sweets we had placed on the table.

Chairwoman Reia and Eighteen were working in another room. I saw some holy knights coming in and out earlier, so I was sure they were still talking about the incident that had occurred this morning.

A little way into our party, I realized I needed to go to the bathroom. I must have had too much fruit juice.

"I'm gonna stop by the bathroom."

I excused myself and left the room. After using the scrupulously clean toilet to take care of my business, I returned to the room to find Lia and the others heavily inebriated.

"Alleeeeen! Welcome baaack!" Lia shouted, waving.

Her speech was slurred, and her cheeks were tinged with red. There was something…amorous in the stare she gave me.

"Th-thanks…," I replied reluctantly.

I quickly scanned the room and found something.

I see, that's what did it…

There was an opened pack of champagne truffles on the table. They must have treated themselves to those alcohol-filled chocolates while I'd been in the restroom.

Two, four, six, eight, ten…geez, fourteen. They had a lot…

I took a quick glance at everyone to assess the damage.

"Bwa-ha-ha-ha-ha! Let's see if you can handle my holy sword Excalibur!"

"My Aegis Shield blocks all attacks, you know…"

Lilim and Tirith were holding pillows and shouting complete nonsense.

Well…that's normal behavior for them.

Their red faces indicated that they were drunk, but that was also how they always acted. It was probably fine to leave them alone.

Rose was sitting on her knees in front of the table, sipping tea. She looked totally unaffected; she might have been the only one not to have partaken in the alcoholic chocolates.

I then turned my gaze to the biggest problems—Lia and Shii. They were both flushed and talking to each other cheerfully...but something about their behavior was clearly abnormal and reeked of imminent danger.

Anyway, I should talk to Rose. She seems to have her head on straight...

I sat down next to her and started speaking.

"Hey, Rose, are the champagne truffles to blame for this?"

"Yeah. I didn't expect them all to be this bad with alcohol... Things got out of hand quickly."

"Did you not eat any, Rose?"

"No, I ate some. They were delicious. There are a lot of heavy drinkers in my family, so I hold my liquor extremely well."

"W-wow..."

Our conversation was then interrupted.

"Allen, open wiiiiide! Lesh eat togetherrr!"

"Allen, you don't want to miss out on these delicious chocolates. My head feels so light... Hmm-hmm, I'm having so much fun."

Flushed, Lia and Shii both grabbed a champagne truffle each and held it in front of my mouth.

Oh my god...

The smell of alcohol and their sweet, girly scents tickled my nose and quickened my pulse.

Lia had let her pigtails down, which was already a fresh look; it combined with the effects of the liquor to give her an unspeakable allure.

On the other hand, the president's snow-white skin was flushed slightly crimson, and her behavior was even warmer and friendlier than usual. She simultaneously had the beauty of a seductress and a loveliness that invited a desire to keep her safe.

And on top of that, they were crawling toward me on all fours in their loose-fitting *yukata*, exposing a significant amount of skin and even their bras. It was a sight I absolutely should not have been privy to.

Th-this is too much...

I felt like I wasn't far from totally losing my mind.

"Allen, won't you have one? For me?" pestered Lia.

"Open your mouth wide, Allen. Like this—*aaah!*" instructed Shii.

They were pressing me really hard...

"A-aaah..."

Feeling like I had no choice, I did as they commanded and opened my mouth. I felt their slim fingers touch my lips and place the champagne truffles on my tongue.

"Hmm-hmm. How ish it, Allen? Do you like it?" asked Lia.

"Isn't it sweet and warm?" added Shii.

"Y-yeah, it's delicious. Thank you."

Honestly, I was too distracted by their lascivious behavior to notice the taste, but I told them what they wanted to hear in the hope that this would all come to an end.

"I'm glad!" the Student Council president said before suddenly jumping at me.

"P-President?!"

As she pressed her soft bosom against me, her sweet scent seemed to envelop my entire body.

"Stop that, P-President... Allen is my master!"

Undaunted, Lia joined Shii on top of me.

"Y-you too, Lia?!"

I was pinned to the floor with Lia on my right and Shii on my left.

"Eh-hee-hee, you smell so nice!" Lia exclaimed.

"Wow, you're so muscular...," Shii said, admiring me.

"..."

I couldn't take any more. This was way too much for my brain to handle.

"R-Rose... Help me!"

I squeezed out the last of my fading strength to plead for rescue, but then I noticed something.

"*Haaah...*"

"*Zzz...*"

Lia and the Student Council president were both breathing softly in their sleep—the liquor had knocked them out.

It's over...

Using my iron will to repress my bodily urges, I somehow managed to escape their clutches.

I glanced around to see Lilim and Tirith each holding a pillow and sleeping. They'd been drunk after all.

"Geez...I'm exhausted..." I sighed loudly.

"Ha, that was a catastrophe," Rose said with a strained laugh.

She'd gotten up to help me out.

"Anyway, champagne truffles are banned starting today."

"Yeah, that's a good idea."

Rose and I carried our wasted friends back to their rooms. Given the late hour, we decided to retire to our own as well.

"*Phew...* That was fun, but really rough at the end..."

I stretched and glanced at the clock on the wall after returning to my room.

"It's already eleven... I need to hit the hay."

Staying up too late would have a negative effect on my performance the following day. I got ready for bed, and right when I turned off the lights, someone knocked on my door.

Who could it be this late at night?

"Who is it?" I asked, opening the door.

"Hey, Allen, sorry for bothering you so late."

It was Chairwoman Reia, crossing her arms and wearing a stern expression.

"What is it, Chairwoman?"

"I have some things to inform you concerning the group that attacked Lia this morning. I know it's late, but could I have a moment of your time?"

"...Yes, ma'am."

They must have uncovered something unnerving about the assailants.

I really just want to go to sleep, but I guess I have no choice...

A valuable friend of mine was in danger. If there was anything I could do to help her, I was going to do it.

I followed the chairwoman to her room. It was surprisingly orderly, without a single loose article of clothing or bottle of spirits in sight.

"I want you to take a look at this first. It'll be faster than trying to explain it to you," she said.

Reia pulled a brown envelope out of her desk that was labeled *Important Document.*

"What's this?"

"This is a report that the holy knights delivered earlier tonight. It's a bit long, so do your best to skim and pick out the crucial parts."

"Yes, ma'am."

I took the report out of the opened brown envelope and began to read it.

Investigation into the Incident in Karlos District, Veneria Island

July 1, Afternoon: Upon investigation, it has been determined that the fifty individuals arrested are assassins from the Holy Ronelian Empire. An inspection of their confiscated weapons confirms this beyond a shadow of a doubt. The assassins all possessed soul-crystal pills, which explicitly connects the Holy Ronelian Empire to the Black Organization.

July 1, Evening: The condition of the criminals took a turn for the worse as a result of the side effects of the soul-crystal pills. Veneria Branch's relief squad is incapable of treatment. We've decided to transfer them to a nearby hospital with the utmost security.

July 1, Night: During transport, an unknown actor slaughtered every one of the criminals, then scrupulously burned all fifty of their bodies. The assailant likely did this to conceal information about the soul-crystal pills that their corpses would have otherwise revealed.

"The whole group was murdered?"

"That's right. They were assassins from either the Holy Ronelian Empire or the Black Organization. The holy knights who'd been guarding the transport were found knocked out."

She shrugged and continued:

"An investigation of the scene of the initial crime found some unexplained footprints near the beach shack. It looks like there was a small group there that was separate from the one that attacked you."

"Really?" I asked.

Chairwoman Reia nodded.

"This incident was almost certainly a combat experiment to test the soul-crystal pills. The enemy prepared two groups—one containing fifty sacrificial pawns, and the second to collect combat data."

"S-sacrificial pawns... Do they really treat human lives so lightly?"

"That is how inhumane the masterminds behind this incident are. You need to watch yourself."

The chairwoman brought the topic to a close with that warning.

"Why are you only telling me this? Shouldn't we let Lia, Rose, and the others know?"

"Because you— Well, I've said enough."

"...?"

"Just trust that I have my reasons. I decided that it was best to inform only you. I expect you to keep mum on what I've told you here."

"R-really? Yes, ma'am..."

I didn't like it, but it didn't seem like she was willing to give me any more information, so I gave her my consent for now.

"That said, there's no need to worry about it too much at present. Know that you'll all be safe whenever I'm around. I'm much stronger than I look."

"Thank you very much."

I'd learned of many tales about Reia's power lately. It was reassuring to hear her say that.

"That's it for now. Sorry for summoning you so late. We still have a bit of training camp left, so make sure to rest up."

"Yes, ma'am. Good night, Chairwoman."

"Night."

I left her room, then returned to mine and entered a deep sleep.

■

After a few more days of training sessions and matches between the Thousand Blade and Ice King students, the final day of our joint summer training camp arrive at last. We dragged our exhausted bodies to the usual gathering spot of Ferris's private beach.

Chairwoman Reia, Ferris, and Shii stood in front of the students.

"Congratulations on making it through this exciting and challenging training camp!" announced Chairwoman Reia.

"You all have worked very hard," added Ferris.

"Let's take this time to enjoy ourselves!" proclaimed Shii.

We'd finally gotten a free day to spend on our last day of training camp.

"Whooo! We can finally get in the ocean!" yelled Lilim.

"This year's training camp was really hard…," complained Tirith.

"Hooray! Let's go have some fun!" shouted an Ice King Academy student.

The students from both Thousand Blade and Ice King cheered loudly. Everyone was overjoyed. Or rather, everyone but me.

It's already over… I wanted to keep practicing with everyone.

I enjoyed swinging my sword by myself, of course, but doing it with everyone else was more fun. It was the same as eating by yourself versus eating in the company of others. I had mixed emotions.

A couple of voices pulled me out of my thoughts.

"Hey, Allen! Do you have a moment?"

"It's so impressive that you can compete with Shido as a first-year!"

Two female Ice King Academy students who looked like upperclassmen had surrounded me.

"Th-thank you."

Bewildered, I was unsure of how to respond.

"Wow, you have such a nice body!"

"Your stomach is hard as a rock!"

Standing to either side of me, the girls started enthusiastically feeling my stomach.

"Huh? Wh-what are—?"

The feeling of their slim fingers touching my skin was so ticklish that I was struggling to speak. I had no idea what to do.

"H-hey, you're clearly bothering Allen!"

"Don't cling to him like that."

Lia and Rose shoved them aside and came up beside me.

"Let's go, Allen!"

"Let's get in the water. It'll be fun."

"Y-yeah, sure."

With both of them in a huff for reasons that had gone over my head, they led me to the beach.

■

Now that the rigid practice sessions of the last few days were over, I could once again appreciate the breathtaking beauty of the ocean.

The majority of the students on the trip were already enjoying themselves on the beach. Some were fishing by the shore, some were building sandcastles, and others were splashing water on one another in the shallows. Everyone was enjoying the final day of summer training camp to the fullest.

"What do you want to do?" I asked casually.

"I've given that some thought—how about this?" Lia asked, showing us three deflated swim rings. She had been carrying them under an arm. "I borrowed these from Shii this morning! I think floating on these in the ocean would be really fun!"

"The current is calm here, and the salty breeze will feel good," said Rose.

They both looked to me for my agreement.

"Sure, sounds like a great idea."

"Yay!"

"Let's get these ready!"

We inflated the swim rings, then got in the water.

"Wow, this is so different from river water!" I observed.

It felt like the ocean was sticking slightly to my skin.

"*Mmm*, it's cold!"

"Yeah, it feels so good."

Since they'd both experienced the sea plenty of times before, they took more pleasure in its coldness than the way it felt. We had fun chatting as we rocked back and forth on the waves in our swim rings.

"You'll never believe what happened next! My father mistook that letter for a confession, so he got all red in the face and shouted, 'If you want my daughter's hand, go prove that you're the greatest swordsman in all the kingdom!'"

Lia was telling us a story about a hilarious misunderstanding that her father—the king of Vesteria—had made.

"Ah-ha-ha, that's funny," I said, chuckling.

"Hmm-hmm, that guy had no idea how to respond."

Talking in this novel environment was so engrossing that I lost track of time. We floated for quite a while.

"...I want to get some practice swings in."

Eventually, a desire to flourish my blade welled up from within me.

It could be interesting swinging my sword without having my feet on the ground.

How could I move my blade in order to achieve even sharper slashes? I wanted to experiment a bit to find out.

"Ha-ha, you really like waving your sword around," said Lia.

"You think about swordcraft literally all the time," added Rose.

"R-really? You're making me blush...," I responded.

""Don't take that as a compliment!"" they both yelled.

We enjoyed our fill of the ocean, until something unexpected happened.

"Eek!"

"H-huh?!"

A large object suddenly burst to the surface of the water, causing Lia and Rose's swim rings to flip over.

"Wh-what the—?!"

I strained my eyes to see what it was.

"Ha-ha! I've caught today's dinner!"

"That was incredible, Shido! I can't believe you caught two fish with your bare hands!"

It was Shido and Cain. Shido was holding two fish in his hands, while Cain was gazing at him in awe.

"Shido, Cain?! What are you doing?!" I asked.

"Huh? …Oh, it's you, Allen," Shido responded.

"Lord Allen! I am so terribly sorry for surprising you. We're free diving. It's really fun!"

It sounded like they were just having a good time in the water.

"Wh-what is wrong with you two?! Can't you come up more gently?!"

"You took us completely off guard!"

Lia and Rose both started grousing after climbing back onto their rings.

"Oh, shut up, you idiots! Speed is essential for catching fish!" Shido yelled.

"Now, now, Shido. That's true when hunting, but that kind of velocity is totally unnecessary when surfacing. Let's be more careful from now on," Cain chided.

"Tch, it's always something…," Shido grumbled to himself. Despite his words, he bowed his head slightly. It seemed like his surprisingly gentle side was coming out again.

"Lord Allen, Lia, Rose. My humble apologies for bothering you. We will see you later," Cain apologized.

"Bye," added Shido.

The two of them went back underwater, enjoying the southern resort in their own unorthodox way.

Once we were done with our inflatables, we joined up with the upperclassmen from the Student Council and had a great rest of the day.

■

That night, we held a barbecue with everyone from Ice King Academy. The party was in front of Ferris's villa at seven at night. After a day of fun, I headed there with my classmates.

"W-wow, check that out!" I exclaimed.

A grand assortment of luxurious foods had been set up, including thick marbled beef, healthily fattened fresh fish, colorful fruits and vegetables, and more.

"It looks delicious!" exclaimed Lia.

"This is going to be incredible!" agreed Rose.

They were both raring to go.

"That's high-quality meat. It's going to taste amazing grilled!" remarked Shii.

"I can't wait for the roast fish! It's the best grilled with salt!" gushed Lilim.

"The fruit seems crazy good...," admired Tirith.

The upperclassmen also looked like they couldn't wait to chow down.

Ferris, who'd been in charge of planning the barbecue, snapped her fan to get everyone's attention.

"Welcome, guests from Thousand Blade Academy. All this is ready to go—so let's dig in!"

Many of the students began to cheer.

"Hooray! Meat!"

"You're the best, Chairwoman Ferris! I love you!"

"I'm gonna pig out today!"

Lia, Rose, and I thanked Ferris, then began to pick food off the table. Once we filled our plates, we went to a four-person table.

"All right."

"Sorry, can you scoot over a bit?"

"S-sure..."

Confusingly, Lia and Rose both sat down next to me.

You aren't supposed to cram three people on one side of this kind of table, but...whatever.

I pierced the marbled beef with a skewer, then placed it on the wire-mesh grill in the middle of the table.

That smells so good...

The fat of the meat sizzled on the grill, and the savory scent tickled my nostrils, fanning my appetite.

Turning to my side, I saw Lia working like an assembly line, filling skewer after skewer with meat and laying them on the grill. No surprises there.

Rose, on the other hand, had a very balanced approach. She put an equal amount of meat and vegetables on her skewers and was grilling a fish alongside them.

Two minutes later, the food looked finished. It was time to indulge.

"Let's eat!"

"Yeah, they're ready!"

"My mouth is watering."

We each reached out for a skewer.

"Stop, you bastards!"

Shido, who happened to be passing by, suddenly snatched the fish skewer out of Lia's hands.

"Sh-Shido?!"

"What the heck are you doing?!"

"What did you do that for?"

We were all taken aback.

"Geez, I knew it. This is menorkasago..."

He clicked his tongue and tossed the fish in the trash.

"M-menorkasago?!"

"Th-that's extremely poisonous!"

"Stop, everyone! Don't eat the fish!"

A commotion broke out among the students. I was pretty sure I'd heard that menorkasago was a fish with a deadly paralytic poison.

"Madam, how could you let this happen?!" Shido pressed Ferris.

"Th-that's strange… I showed all our catch to a local fisherman, and he said that none of them were toxic…," she muttered apologetically.

"Tch, can't trust goddamn anybody… Hey, bring me all the fish! No one eats them without the Shido stamp of approval!"

He then set to rapidly checking each one of the many catches packed into the cooler.

"Shido knows a lot about seafood," I remarked.

Cain overheard me and launched into an explanation.

"That he does. I would even go so far as to call him a fish expert. Shido apparently grew up in a very unique environment, where he gained an expansive knowledge of survival skills. If you could only take one thing to a deserted island, I recommend you take him."

"I-interesting…"

I wondered what Shido's childhood had been like. He was a mysterious person. But regardless, he'd saved us yet again.

"Thank you very much for saving Lia, Shido," I said.

"Thanks, that was really close," said Lia.

"You have my thanks as well," added Rose.

The three of us gave our appreciation to him in turn.

"Geez, you guys give me the creeps. Don't get the wrong idea, trash babies. I wasn't out to save you; I just happened to see it."

He responded in his typically standoffish manner and turned away in a huff. He was always foulmouthed, but I believed he was a good person deep down.

We all returned to our seats and restarted the barbecue after collecting ourselves. Shido was checking the seafood, so we ate the meat and vegetables.

"This is so good!"

"These onions are so sweet, and perfectly chewy!"

"This food was provided by the famed House Dorhein, after all. It's top-notch grub through and through!"

As we enjoyed the meals together, a large firework suddenly burst in the night sky.

"Wow, a firework!"

"How beautiful…"

"It's so elegant…"

The red, blue, and green multicolored firework was striking on the black canvas of the sky behind it.

"Allen, Rose, let's go to summer training camp again next year," insisted Lia.

"For sure," I responded.

"Of course," said Rose.

The joint summer training camp between Thousand Blade Academy and Ice King Academy certainly had its ups and downs, but we got through it just fine in the end.

CHAPTER 5

The Vesteria Royal Guard

Our private jet arrived at the Arkstoria mansion at seven in the morning the next day.

"Thank you for everything, President. That was a really great experience."

"Thank you very much. It was a lot of fun!"

"*Yawn...* Thanks."

I expressed my gratitude to her alongside Lia and Rose.

"Hmm-hmm, you're very welcome. See you at the academy," Shii responded with a kind smile.

Chairwoman Reia, who'd traveled back with us, cleared her throat.

"You kids will face much temptation during summer break but try not to have *too* much fun!"

She attempted to bring the summer training camp to a close by giving us a very teacher-like warning.

Doesn't hold much weight coming from her, though.

The chairwoman had gotten herself wasted just the previous night by having a drinking contest for the ages with Ferris. We all ignored her with strained smiles.

"Want to head to our dorms?" I proposed.

"Yeah, let's go," responded Lia.

"I need a nap...," said Rose, yawning.

The three of us started to walk back toward the Thousand Blade Academy dorms.

"I'll accompany you partway. I'd normally just return home, but I have an unusual guest today. It's a real pain, but as the chairwoman, I need to meet with them," Reia said with a sigh.

We walked through the winding streets of Aurest, eventually arriving at Thousand Blade Academy. Rose stopped at a corner leading to multiple buildings.

"*Yawn...* My dorm is this way. See you later..."

She rubbed an eye with her left hand and waved with her right.

"Bye, Rose," I said.

"Make sure you don't oversleep in the morning," cautioned Lia.

"Take care of yourself!" the chairwoman added.

We continued on to the dorm where Lia and I lived in. A nice breeze blew past us.

"The wind feels so good."

"It really does."

"I couldn't agree more!"

After a few minutes, I caught sight of a swordsman ahead of us wearing dark-blue, expensive-looking clothes.

That outfit is really fancy. I wonder if he's a noble.

A moment later, the swordsman did something unexpected.

"Hegemonic Style—Annihilation!"

He rushed toward me and aggressively slashed his blade.

"Huh?!"

I drew my weapon and blocked the move just in the nick of time.

Geez, he's strong...

From the incredible speed and weight behind his blow, I could tell he was no ordinary swordsman. Intriguingly, he used the same School of Swordcraft as Lia.

"Wh-what is this about?!" I asked.

"Back away from Her Highness, you boorish swine!"

The regal fighter glared at me with a face full of rage.

Did he say Her Highness?

"C-Claude?! What are you doing here?!" asked Lia.

"Hey, long time no see, Claude!" greeted the chairwoman.

They both seemed to know him.

His angry eyes were piercing and sharp. His black, glossy hair was a little long, and he wore resplendent clothes typical of the nobility. I guessed he was around fifteen years old. At about 165 centimeters tall, he was slightly shorter than me.

"Um...could you please introduce us, Lia?" I asked.

"Ah, sorry. This is Claude Stroganof, the captain of the Vesteria Royal Guard. I thought the Royal Guard was busy with their duties at home...," Lia told me.

"I—I see..."

I didn't know why he'd assaulted me out of the blue, but I supposed he was an ally.

"It's so nice to see you again, Your Highness! Reia, explain yourself! How could you let such a filthy maggot get near her?!"

"Filthy maggot"?

We hadn't even said a word to each other yet... Talk about uncalled for.

Chairwoman Reia shook her head in disbelief in response to Claude's reprimand.

"Cool your jets, Claude. These two have a...special relationship," she said.

"S-special, you say?! D-don't tell me...a-are they l-l-l-overs?!" stammered Claude, pale-faced and trembling.

"Oh, no. It's much more extreme than that. Their relationship is one of master and servant—put bluntly, she's his slave."

The chairwoman revealed the shocking truth.

"Princess Lia...is a slave? ...Huh?"

Claude's face went totally blank.

"Ch-Chairwoman?!"

"R-Reia?! Why did you tell Claude that?!"

"Ha-ha-ha! What would be the point in lying?"

She burst out laughing.

I can't believe her!

The maniac was totally enjoying this.

Crap, how can we talk our way out of this?!

We were speaking with the captain of the Vesteria Royal Guard. I couldn't begin to imagine the trouble that would occur if he knew that Lia was "under my command."

"Y-Your Highness…is this true?" he asked Lia directly.

This is our chance!

If she just gave a firm *no*, that would put an end to this nonsense. Chairwoman Reia's horrible transgression would come to nothing!

But that's not what she did.

"Um, well…y-yeah, it is…"

Instead, she blushed and nodded.

Well…honesty is one of her virtues…

That was a good trait for anyone to have, and I didn't want her to change that about herself.

Time and place, though! Time and place!

In this situation, a white lie would have been best.

Lia's confirmation of the awful truth may as well have been a spear through Claude's heart.

"Y-you can't be… Princess Lia… A slave…?"

The shock was so great that he fainted on the spot.

"C-Claude?! Get up, Claude!" Lia yelled.

"Ha-ha-ha, this is about to get real interesting!" the chairwoman guffawed, clapping me on the back.

…This is bad. This is the worst situation I've faced yet.

I'd enslaved the princess of a nation, even if I didn't treat her as such. That was a big deal. To make matters worse, I'd heard that Lia's father was as overprotective as they came.

Ugh…why do these things always happen to me…?

I heaved a huge side and stared up at the blue sky.

■

Afterward, Chairwoman Reia carried the unconscious Claude to the academy's infirmary. The nurse told us he had symptoms of anemia brought on by significant stress, but he would wake soon after some rest. When she asked the chairwoman what happened, the nurse received the vague answer that he'd "received some shocking news."

We waited for about ten minutes before Claude stirred.

"Urgh…where am I…?"

He slowly opened his eyes in the bed he had been placed in.

"Ah, you're awake!" Lia exclaimed.

"Y-Your Highness? Thank goodness. Everything was just a vision after all…," mumbled Claude.

"…Huh?"

He smiled softly with relief.

"It was the strangest dream… You'd left to study abroad and had become the slave of some repulsive maggot… What a horrible nightmare."

"U-um…that wasn't a dream."

"What do you mean? …Huh?!"

Claude's gaze darted around the room and landed on me.

"You're the maggot! No, that was all real…"

He jumped out of bed and glared at me with a mixture of animosity and outright loathing.

"Nice to meet you, Claude. I'm Allen Rodol."

I wasn't really a fan of being compared to vermin, so I decided to give him my name. I didn't get the response I was looking for, though.

"I couldn't care less about your name, you savage pig! Stay away from Princess Lia!"

He stared at me with total hostility. I could see I wasn't going to be able to have a conversation with him.

Wh-what should I do…?

I wanted to keep the information he'd learned between us. It was of the utmost importance that we avoided the king of Vesteria finding out about the nature of the relationship between Lia and me.

I need to get him to talk to me somehow…

I sighed internally. This was obviously going to be difficult.

"How dare you, Claude! You're going too far with your words! Apologize to Allen!" Lia snapped, clearly offended.

"Y-Your Highness? You trust this filthy maggot completely, don't you...?" Claude gritted his teeth, visibly trembling after Lia's scolding. "You've always been a little clumsy... He must be deceiving you somehow!"

"W-wanna repeat that?!"

Claude ignored Lia and continued to glare at me.

"Remember this, maggot! I'm going to give you hell to pay! And, Your Highness...I promise to free you from his evil clutches! For now, we part. I'll see you again soon."

He then jumped out of the infirmary window.

"...*Pfft*, ha-ha-ha! Claude never fails to crack me up! I've always enjoyed teasing that lunkhead!"

Chairwoman Reia had been fighting hard to keep a straight face, but the moment Claude left, she grabbed her stomach and burst out with laughter.

"Ugh...Chairwoman?"

"R-Reia! What the hell are you trying to do here?!"

"Hmm-hmm, don't give me that look. It was just a little prank."

But the repercussions of this would greatly surpass the level of a "little prank"...

"*Phew*... Getting serious for a moment, Claude will most likely try to approach Allen before long. At that point, you'll have a choice—explain the full situation to show there's no problem or fabricate a story to cover it up."

"Both of those options sound like a pain...," I responded.

Claude had looked like he was going to erupt with fury. I didn't think he was going to listen to us.

"You'll just have to do your best! Anyway, that's my business taken care of, so I'm off!"

The chairwoman swiveled and left the infirmary. It seemed that Claude was the unusual guest she'd mentioned earlier.

"Haah…we should head home, too," I said, sighing.

"Claude could strike, anywhere, day or night… You need to be careful, Allen," Lia warned.

"Will do."

We left the infirmary and returned to our dorm.

■

A full day passed without any sign of Claude.

I can't let my guard down, though.

He was probably planning his attack at this very moment. I needed to be ready for him at all times.

"Man…guess I'll head back."

It was seven in the morning. I finished my daily morning practice swings and returned to the dorm.

"*Yawn…* Oh, morning, Allen. You're up early again."

Lia gave me a drowsy wave, still in her pajamas. She must have just woken up.

"Good morning, Lia. Oh yeah, you got a letter."

I handed her the envelope I found in our mailbox.

"For me? Who's it from?"

"I dunno. There's no name on it."

Somebody must have dropped it directly into our mailbox.

"Oh no!"

There was a bombastic red seal on the back of the envelope.

"Wh-what is it?" I asked.

"This is a letter from my father…," she answered.

"Your father… Do you mean the king of Vesteria?!"

"Yeah. This doesn't bode well…"

This could only be about one thing. Claude must have returned and reported to the king immediately.

"Well…won't know until we read it."

"Y-yeah…"

She opened the envelope carefully and took out a folded, high-quality piece of paper. The following was written on the letter in neat handwriting.

> *To my beloved Lia,*
>
> *I heard an interesting story from Claude. It sounds like you're having trouble adjusting to your new environment. In fact, I've been so worried that I haven't been able to focus on my duties. How about you return home for summer break?*
> *I've sent a royal aircraft to arrive at Thousand Blade Academy on July 6 at ten in the morning. Make sure you bring your friend Allen Rodol with you. I can't wait to meet him.*
>
> *I love you.*
>
> *From,*
>
> *Papa*

At first glance, the letter seemed nice and innocent. However, the hidden anger oozing from his words was plain to see.

"F-Father is really pissed..."

"Yeah, that's pretty clear..."

He had just learned that his beloved daughter, whom he'd allowed to study abroad, had become a slave to some guy he knew nothing about. It was a natural reaction.

Claude being the one to report this is only made matters worse.

I was sure he'd embellished the story as much as he could.

"Wh-what should we do, Allen?! July sixth is today!"

"...We have no choice but to go."

This was the king of a nation we were dealing with. He was bound to be a much wiser and more mature person than Claude. I was sure he would understand if we gave him the full story.

"S-sorry about this... I've given you nothing but grief," Lia apologized.

"Don't worry about it. We need to focus on preparing for this trip. Time is already running short."

"Y-yeah, you're right... Thanks."

Lia ran into the dressing room.

"Geez...I can't believe this..."

Receiving a direct summons from a king was quite overwhelming for a simple student like me.

First, Veneria Island, and now across the sea to Vesteria Kingdom... I'm not going to get any rest this summer vacation, am I...?

Sighing, I began to pack for the trip.

Afterword

To everyone who picked up Volume 2 of *100-Million-Year Button*, thank you very much! I'm the author, Syuichi Tsukishima.

I would like to touch briefly on the content of this novel. This will contain spoilers, so those who read the afterword first should be careful.

Volume 2 is composed of three parts: the witchblade section, the Club-Budget War section, and the summer-training-camp section. Finally, I added the Vesteria Kingdom component at the end to set up the next part of the story. I think this turned out to be a pretty dense novel.

The addition of some new characters helped me spruce up the dialogue, and I inserted many battles throughout. I really hope you all enjoyed it.

Volume 3 will contain a few more arcs, including the part of the story that takes place in Lia's homeland of Vesteria Kingdom. I promise it will be even more jam-packed than Volume 2!

(The release date is planned for a few months from now! It's going to be a very fun entry, so please look forward to it!)

Now I'd like to give some thanks.

To the illustrator, Mokyu, thank you very much for your brilliant character designs and your many adorable illustrations. Thank you as well to the lead editor for all their help, the proofreader for fixing typos, and everyone else who worked on this book.

And more than anything, thank you very much to every reader who's picked up Volume 2 of *100-Million-Year Button*.

May we meet again in volume 3.

The DetectiVe Is AlreadY Dead

When the story begins without its hero

Kimihiko Kimizuka has always been a magnet for trouble and intrigue. For as long as he can remember, he's been stumbling across murder scenes or receiving mysterious attaché cases to transport. When he met Siesta, a brilliant detective fighting a secret war against an organization of pseudohumans, he couldn't resist the call to become her assistant and join her on an epic journey across the world.

...Until a year ago, that is. Now he's returned to a relatively normal and tepid life, knowing the adventure must be over. After all, the detective is already dead.

Volume 1 available wherever books are sold!

 YEN ON

TANTEI HA MO, SHINDEIRU. Vol. 1
©nigozyu 2019
Illustration: Umibouzu
KADOKAWA CORPORATION